DOWN FROM THE SHIMMERING SKY
MASKS OF THE NORTHWEST COAST

PETER MACNAIR   ROBERT JOSEPH   BRUCE GRENVILLE

DOUGLAS & McINTYRE

VANCOUVER/TORONTO

UNIVERSITY OF WASHINGTON PRESS

SEATTLE

VANCOUVER ART GALLERY

Copyright © 1998 by Vancouver Art Gallery
"Behind the Mask" copyright © 1998 by Robert Joseph
"Power of the Shining Heavens" copyright © 1998 by Peter Macnair

99 00 01 02   5 4 3

Douglas & McIntyre Ltd.
2323 Québec Street, Suite 201
Vancouver, British Columbia V5T 4S7

Canadian Cataloguing in Publication Data
Macnair, Peter L.
Down from the shimmering sky

Based on an exhibition at the Vancouver Art Gallery.
ISBN 1-55054-623-6

1. Indian masks—Northwest Coast of North America—Exhibitions. I. Joseph, Robert. II. Grenville, Bruce. III. Vancouver Art Gallery. IV. Title.
E78.N78M32 1998   731'.75'0899707111   C98-910006-5

Editing by Saeko Usukawa
Design by George Vaitkunas
Front cover: detail of *Mask Representing the Sun*, c. 1870, Nuxalk, Artist Unknown, 160.0 diameter, wood and paint, courtesy American Museum of Natural History, New York, 16/1507, photograph by Trevor Mills, Vancouver Art Gallery
Printed and bound in Canada by Friesens
Printed on acid-free paper

Printed on Bravo Dull 100 lb. text from E.B. Eddy Paper

The publisher gratefully acknowledges the support of the Canada Council for the Arts and of the British Columbia Ministry of Tourism, Small Business and Culture. The publisher also acknowledges the financial support of the Government of Canada through the Book Publishing Industry Development Program for our publishing activities.

Originated in Canada by Douglas & McIntyre and the Vancouver Art Gallery, and published simultaneously in the United States of America by the University of Washington Press, P.O. Box 50096, Seattle, WA 98145-5096

Library of Congress Cataloging-in-Publication Date

Macnair, Peter L.
   Down from the shimmering sky : masks of the Northwest Coast / Peter Macnair, Robert Joseph, Bruce Grenville.
      p. cm.
   Includes bibliographical references.
   ISBN 0-295-97709-4 (alk. paper)
   1. Indian masks—Northwest Coast of North America—Exhibitions. I. Joseph, Robert, 1939-   . II. Grenville, Bruce. III. Title.
E78.N78M32   1998
731'.75'089970795—dc21   98-15997
                                                              CIP

The paper used in this publication meets the minimum requirements of American National Standard for Information Sciences—Permanence of Paper for Printed Library Materials, ANSI Z39.48-1984.

All measurements are in centimetres: height precedes width precedes depth.

1 (frontispiece)
Nisga'a, Artist Unknown
Mask Representing the Moon, 19th century
35.4 × 25.6 × 15.3
cedar, nails and paint
Royal British Columbia Museum, Victoria, 9694
Photo by Trevor Mills, Vancouver Art Gallery

CONTENTS

DIRECTOR'S FOREWORD

ONE OF THE PRINCIPAL MANDATES of the Vancouver Art Gallery is to exhibit and document the diverse arts of British Columbia. In doing so, we produce a rich visual history of our environment and the people who inhabit it. Where once our audience might have been said to be largely limited to the City of Vancouver and the people of the Lower Mainland, today the art of this region has a strong national and international constituency. Nowhere is this more evident than in the public's interest in the art of the First Nations of the Pacific Northwest Coast. The scope of this exhibition, which will travel throughout North America, and this outstanding publication are an acknowledgement of the important role the Vancouver Art Gallery plays in disseminating the art of this place to a broad and attentive audience.

Down from the Shimmering Sky is the first large-scale, survey exhibition on the subject of the masks of the Northwest Coast; it offers an opportunity to see rare and exceptional material that, in some instances, left this coast more than two hundred years ago. A number of these works, housed in public collections in Germany, Switzerland, Austria, the United States, Canada and elsewhere, represent some of the earliest masks collected by foreign explorers, traders and government officials. These pieces offer a context for the remaining masks, both historical and contemporary, that come from the many excellent public collections, First Nations cultural centres and private collections of this region. We are proud to be able to offer this comprehensive overview of the historical and contemporary mask-making traditions of the Northwest Coast.

We would like to express our gratitude to our guest curators Peter Macnair and Robert Joseph for the extraordinary efforts they have made in organizing this exhibition, and to all of the staff at the Vancouver Art Gallery and Douglas & McIntyre who have contributed to making this project a success. We would also like to thank all the lenders, both institutional and private, who agreed to part with their masks for this exhibition and tour.

This project has made an extraordinary demand on the gallery's resources, and we would like to acknowledge the sponsors, patrons and members of the Board of Trustees who directly supported this project and contributed to its success. We thank Michael Audain, President of the Board of the Vancouver Art Gallery, for his initial and ongoing enthusiasm and backing. We are extremely grateful to the Scotiabank for its substantial assistance and are proud of their support. The Vancouver Sun, CBC British Columbia, and Metropolitan Fine Printers Inc. provided the means for publicizing this rare event. E.B. Eddy Paper generously supported the production of this book. Finally, we thank the Canada Council for the Arts for its contribution to the research and production of this exhibition and publication.

ALF BOGUSKY
Director, Vancouver Art Gallery

ACKNOWLEDGEMENTS

AN EXHIBITION OF THIS SCALE AND CHARACTER requires the skills and efforts of a great many people and the co-operation and good will of many institutions. First and foremost, we thank the artists who made these many works and the families who have permitted us to display their masks. Their willingness to share their rich cultural heritage has made this exhibition possible. My co-curators Peter Macnair and Robert Joseph have laboured long and hard to bring these masks together and negotiate their use for the exhibition and publication. We at the Vancouver Art Gallery thank them for their efforts and congratulate them on their success. Jay Stewart has been a silent partner in this project, quietly keeping all of the curatorial team on track and on time, and we are grateful to her for her foresight, patience and good humour.

We thank the advisors who represented the Tlingit, Nisga'a, Gitxsan, Tsimshian, Haida, Heiltsuk, Nuxalk, Kwakwaka'wakw, Nuu-chah-nulth, Makah and Coast Salish Nations, lending their knowledge and wisdom to this project. And we thank Gloria Cranmer Webster for her advice. Leona Sparrow and Howard Grant were thoughtful advisors from the Musqueam Band; we appreciate their guidance. We owe special thanks to the Musqueam people, our hosts for this exhibition.

Many artists and private collectors have lent works to us, and we appreciate their generosity and willingness to share these extraordinary masks. Our colleagues at the Royal British Columbia Museum in Victoria have kindly lent a number of important works from their collection, and we acknowledge the substantial demands made on their institution and staff. As well, we are grateful to the curators and staff of the many other institutions who understood the scope and significance of the project and made special efforts to lend their masks: Campbell River Museum, Campbell River; Canadian Museum of Civilization, Hull; McCord Museum of Canadian History, Montreal; McMichael Canadian Art Collection, Kleinburg; Royal Ontario Museum, Toronto; U'mista Cultural Centre, Alert Bay; University of British Columbia Museum of Anthropology, Vancouver; Vancouver Museum, Vancouver; Linden-Museum Stuttgart, Staatliches Museum für Völkerkunde, Stuttgart; Museum für Völkerkunde, Vienna; Museum für Völkerkunde, Berlin; Bernisches Historisches Museum, Bern; American Antiquarian Society, Worcester; American Museum of Natural History, New York; Field Museum, Chicago; National Museum of Natural History Smithsonian Institution, Washington; Milwaukee Public Museum, Milwaukee; Peabody Essex Museum and the Phillips Library, Salem; Peabody Museum of Archeology & Ethnology, Harvard University, Cambridge; Portland Museum of Art, Portland; Seattle Art Museum, Seattle; University of Pennsylvania Museum of Archeology & Anthropology, Philadelphia. Finally, we thank our colleagues at the Portland Art Museum, Portland, the Gilcrease Museum, Tulsa, and the National Museum of the American Indian, New York, who supported this project by participating in the tour of this exhibition.

At the Vancouver Art Gallery, the entire staff has contributed to this project, and many of them have made exceptional efforts to ensure its success. Our registrar, Helle Viirlaid, has patiently negotiated with museums across Canada, the United States and Europe to safely bring these masks back to their point of origin, and we appreciate her commitment. Photographer Trevor Mills seized the opportunity to direct his considerable skills to the documentation of this work, and we thank him for his splendid images. Glen Flanderka, Bruce Wiedrick, Paula O'Keefe and the preparation staff willingly and skillfully tackled the myriad problems that arose in mounting the exhibition. Jacqueline Chiang and Lynne Kelman co-ordinated mounds of paperwork with patience and skill. Our special thanks to Director Alf Bogusky, Chief Curator and Associate Director Daina Augaitis, Ian Thom, Grant Arnold, Kitty Scott, Angela Mah, Cheryl Meszaros, Nancy Kirkpatrick, Janet Meredith, Colette Warburton, Sanam Bakhtiar, Cheryl Siegel, Allister Brown, Monica Smith, Lenore Swenerton, Louise McCall, Sharon Young and Tom Collins.

It has been a pleasure to work with Douglas & McIntyre, which embraced this project despite an already active publishing schedule. Their efforts and example set high standards for us to meet. We thank publisher Scott McIntyre, editor Saeko Usukawa and designer George Vaitkunas for bringing their considerable skills to this book and ensuring its success.

This project would not have been possible without the backing of a number of sponsors. Notably, the generous support of Scotiabank has ensured the exhibition's success. Our media sponsors, The Vancouver Sun and CBC British Columbia; print sponsor Metropolitan Fine Printers Inc.; paper sponsor E.B. Eddy Paper and the Canada Council for the Arts have made substantial contributions. We are grateful to all of them for their assistance.

BRUCE GRENVILLE
Senior Curator

CURATORS' STATEMENT

Images seem to speak to the eye, but they are really addressed to the mind. They are ways of thinking, in the guise of ways of seeing. The eye can sometimes be satisfied with form alone, but the mind can only be satisfied with meaning, which can be contemplated, more consciously or less, after the eye is closed. —Wilson Duff

THESE PROVOCATIVE WORDS from Northwest Coast scholar Wilson Duff introduce *Images Stone B.C.*, an exhibition featured at the Vancouver Art Gallery in 1975, as well as the associated catalogue.[1] The exhibit addressed a three-thousand-year span of stone sculpture from the Northwest Coast of North America, and Duff offered some daring insights into the meaning and metaphor of an ancient artistic tradition which continues, unbroken, today.

Our journey to discover and celebrate this abiding sculptural tradition in the less enduring medium of wood proceeds from the silent stone. In the show's catalogue, Duff reflected upon and illustrated a pair of stone masks, one sighted and the other unsighted, which were the transcendent works in his exhibition. The sighted twin has eyes which are simple circular holes pecked through the stone. The unsighted twin (Figure 2) has eyes which are convex domes and thus appear to be closed, or "unsighted."[2] Although their age is unknown, these two stone masks have long been considered ultimate masterpieces, reflecting the epitome of form and presence which characterize the best of Northwest Coast art. They celebrate the maker's genius and serve to look both backward and forward in time, seeing and not seeing, revealing and concealing, providing an enigma which we can never completely fathom.

As Duff indicates, the eye can sometimes be satisfied with form alone. But in order to separate the accomplished from the pedestrian, the eye must be educated. Scholars have provided a basis for this by offering analyses of form which allow the viewer to understand the conventions of line and shape in Northwest Coast art so as to make informed aesthetic judgments.[3]

However, as Duff implies, the viewer must also look beyond form and discover meaning in order to satisfy the intellect. Meaning is revealed through the oral traditions of the First Peoples which define a cosmos inhabited by magical ancestral forces. These powers are represented by masks which make the supernatural world visible. We can only begin to understand and appreciate masks when they are contextualized by the authority of the Native voice.[4]

We can add to our enlightenment by examining the records of the explorers, traders and professional collectors whose interaction with Native peoples on the Northwest Coast spans more than two centuries. Often, they offer insights which are crucial to our understanding of the aesthetic, cultural and historical contexts in which the art was created.

As our study of masks in institutional and private collections advanced, it became evident that there is a large corpus of masks, primarily representing the human face, which were made for sale to Europeans and Americans rather than for use within Native cultures. The earliest examples of these began to appear in numbers in the 1820s. Although these particular masks are known to and have been remarked upon by scholars, as a phenomenon they have not yet been addressed at length. We consider them to be extremely influential in the evolution of a commercial as well as ethnographic tradition and have featured them as a prominent theme.

Attributing undocumented masks from the historic era, or those which have questionable records, is a challenge. In the captions, words or phrases marked with an asterisk (*) indicate a new attribution for the artist, tribal style, type or date of a mask. This attribution has been made by curator Peter Macnair. Note also that all measurements are in centimetres: height precedes width precedes depth.

Many historic masks were not available due to their fragile nature and their commitment to existing or proposed displays, as well as the legitimate sentiments of First Nations people who increasingly are advising museums that certain artifacts must not be exhibited.[5]

The relationship between masks made for traditional use and masks made for sale provided a rationale for selecting works by contemporary artists. Today, there are many more accomplished Northwest Coast artists making masks than could be accommodated in this project; we have included only the work of those artists who have made a substantial contribution to their own culture by producing ceremonial art for the use of their chiefs as well as for the commercial market.

Down from the Shimmering Sky seeks to provide glimpses of the sophisticated culture and the mature artistic tradition experienced by the first foreign venturers to this land and which intrigues us to this day.

PETER L. MACNAIR

ROBERT JOSEPH

BRUCE GRENVILLE

NOTES

1
Wilson Duff, *Images Stone B.C.: Thirty Centuries of Northwest Coast Indian Sculpture*, 12.

2
The sighted stone mask is at the Musée de l'Homme, Paris, collection no. 81.22.1.

3
For an analytical system that allows us to understand, intellectualize and master the two-dimensional art form of the Northwest Coast, see Bill Holm, *Northwest Coast Indian Art: An Analysis of Form*. For helpful guides to understanding the three-dimensional sculptural art form, see Bill Holm, *The Box of Daylight: Northwest Coast Indian Art*; Bill Holm, *The Art and Times of Willie Seaweed* and Peter L. Macnair, Alan Hoover and Kevin Neary, *The Legacy: Continuing Traditions of Northwest Coast Indian Art*.

4
For one of the best contemporary summaries on the issue of art from the Native point of view, see Nora Marks Dauenhauer, "Tlingit At.óow: Traditions and Concepts." She brings a sensitive and informed Tlingit perspective to the issue.

5
For example, in recent years, the Coast Salish have requested that museums remove Sxwaixwe masks from display, as they are employed in rituals that properly should be viewed only by members of the culture.

TLINGIT

Juneau

U.S.A. / CANADA

ALASKA

NISG̲A'A

Old Kasaan

Ketchikan

Kaigani

Tongas

GIT X SAN

Old Massett

Fort Simpson

HAIDA

Prince
Rupert

Kitimat

HAIDA

Kitkatla

HAISLA

Skidegate

TSIMSHIAN

GWAII

(QUEEN
CHARLOTTE
ISLANDS)

HAIHAIS

BRITISH
COLUMBIA

Waglisla

NUXALK

Fort McLoughlin

Bella Coola

HEILTSUK

OWEEKENO

Kingcome
Village

KWAKWA̲KA'WAKW

Fort Rupert

Gilford
Village

Alert Bay

Cape
Mudge

CANADA

Campbell River

COAST

BC

Friendly Cove

VANCOUVER
ISLAND

SALISH

USA

NUU-CHA-NULTH

Port
Alberni

Vancouver

CANADA

Pacific Ocean

U.S.A.

Neah Bay

Victoria

MAKAH

WASHINGTON

0   100 miles

Seattle

0   100 kilometers

INTRODUCTION

BRUCE GRENVILLE

THE FIRST NATIONS of the Pacific Northwest Coast have produced a rich legacy of carved and painted objects as complex and diverse as the histories of the peoples who produced them. Among these objects, the ceremonial mask has long played an integral role in defining and preserving the stories, values, privileges, status and responsibilities of their owners and makers. *Down from the Shimmering Sky: Masks of the Northwest Coast* offers a rare opportunity to explore two centuries of mask making from the hands of the region's finest artists.

Today's community of Northwest Coast mask makers is strong and vital. United by their shared beliefs and traditions, they continue to produce masks of extraordinary diversity and innovation. While the names of the earliest artists have been lost, the masks made by Charles Edenshaw, Willie Seaweed, Mungo Martin, Robert Davidson, Freda Diesing, Richard Hunt, Art Thompson and many others are widely recognized for their quality and invention.

Masks are a manifestation of powerful ancestral spirits and are used to make the supernatural world visible. The earliest masks collected in the late eighteenth and early nineteenth centuries were often human face masks representing spirits that descended from the heavens and assumed human form. Later, masks depicting animals and supernatural creatures became predominant in collectors' closets. These animals and creatures may be represented within the four dimensions of the cosmos as perceived by the First Nations of the Northwest Coast: the Sky World, the Mortal World, the Undersea World and the Spirit World. These five components (the human face mask and the four dimensions of the cosmos) provide the formal and thematic structure of this project. Historical and contemporary masks are shown side by side so that points of continuity and change can be identified. Issues of aesthetics, masks produced for sale, the continuation of and gradual change in forms, personal styles and nontraditional masks are also subthemes explored throughout.

While the historical masks have a strong and formative presence, they are well matched by the character and diversity of the contemporary masks. These latter vary significantly: some are traditional in their technique and subject matter while others seek to extend traditional forms and to use the masks as a medium to explore a broader range of social and political issues. Each of these contemporary masks tells a tale of purpose and expression, striking a calculated balance between tradition and originality.

This exhibition and publication were not intended to compete with the ethnographic projects traditionally mounted by public museums. Nor were they intended—in the tradition of the art gallery—to reduce the mask to a formal aesthetic object largely devoid of meaning or background. Instead, the guest curators, Peter Macnair and Robert Joseph, were given the mandate to create a hybrid project that acknowledged the social and historical context for the production and use of the masks while at the same time documenting their aesthetic and conceptual evolution from the time of first contact with Europeans to the present. They also set themselves the task of locating, where possible, masks that had been used in Potlatch ceremonies or had been danced in public. Thus, many of the masks, both historical and contemporary, have a rich history of use—a history that is manifestly revealed in their scars of repair and replacement. Robert Joseph's absorbing account of the dance from the vantage point of the dancer confirms the role of the mask as a powerful object that seamlessly blends the aesthetic with the social and cultural. His narrative is a timely prescription against the bipolar models of ethnography and connoisscurship that threaten to engulf the study of Northwest Coast arts.

Despite our desire to explore the contextual history of the mask-making tradition, the story would not be complete if we showed only those masks that been used ceremonially. In fact, many of the very old masks were never used in traditional functions, having been traded or sold shortly after being produced. The most famous of these, as Peter Macnair reveals, is the so-called "Jenna Cass" mask that dates from the early nineteenth century and is one of the first masks produced for trade. The practice of making non-ceremonial masks for sale continues today, and many of the innovations that have been brought to the mask-making tradition can be traced to artists' responses to the demands of the commercial market.

The organization of this project has involved an extended curatorial process that acknowledges the strong social and cultural context in which masks are made and used. Guest curators Peter Macnair and Robert Joseph have met with representatives of each of the eleven First Nations of the Pacific Northwest Coast to discuss the project and its goals and to secure support for it. Through this process, we hope to ensure that the privileges and rights associated with individual masks are appropriately protected, that permission to exhibit and document the masks has been granted and that the masks are displayed and represented in a manner that acknowledges their social and ceremonial meaning. In addition, we have elicited the support and guidance of the Musqueam Band, part of the Coast Salish Nation, who, together with the Vancouver Art Gallery, will host the exhibition, in acknowledgement that the gallery is located within Musqueam territory.

Down from the Shimmering Sky: Masks of the Northwest Coast develops a strand of inquiry central to the Vancouver Art Gallery's ongoing commitment to exhibit, collect, document and critically contextualize works by First Nations artists. Past group exhibitions have included the seminal *People of the Potlatch* (1956), *Arts of the Raven: Masterworks by the Northwest Coast Indian* (1967), *Images Stone B.C.: Thirty Centuries of Northwest Coast Indian Sculpture* (1975) and *Beyond History* (1989). Others have featured the work of individuals, including the *Bill Reid Retrospective* (1974), which marked the first time the gallery mounted a solo exhibition of a First Nations artist. More recently, *Robert Davidson: Eagle of the Dawn* (1993) featured a comprehensive overview of work by this master carver, printmaker, painter and jeweller. Still other exhibitions have contextualized the work of regional First Nations artists within the broad range of issues and ideas that inform the production of contemporary art: land, identity, the politics of representation and experimental media are recurrent subjects/issues shared by Native and non-Native artists alike.

Down from the Shimmering Sky provides an important opportunity for the Vancouver Art Gallery to explore and affirm the significant links between historical and contemporary First Nations mask-making traditions. In doing so, we seek to honour a unique cultural and artistic history and to challenge the modernist dogma that innovation can only take place through the rejection of tradition. As guest curators Peter Macnair and Robert Joseph convincingly attest, growth comes from understanding, knowledge and respect. To embrace tradition is not necessarily to reject innovation or experimentation; even a cursory glance at the masks will confirm the dramatic and sometimes convulsive transformations that have occurred. *Down from the Shimmering Sky* is a remarkable and timely survey of the Pacific Northwest Coast mask making that not only will inspire the current generation but, in the tradition of the Northwest Coast First Nations, will inspire and influence generations to come.

3 (facing page)
Kwakwaka'wakw, Bob Harris*
Mask Representing Bakwas,
c. 1890
30.5 × 25.5 × 25.0
red cedar, horsehair, feathers, brass and cloth
U'mista Cultural Centre, Alert Bay, 80.01.013
Photo by Trevor Mills, Vancouver Art Gallery

BEHIND THE MASK

ROBERT JOSEPH

THE MASKS OF THE INDIGENOUS PEOPLES of the Pacific Northwest Coast are powerful objects that assist us in defining our place in the cosmos. In a world of endless change and complexity, masks offer a continuum for Native people to acknowledge our connection to the universe.

This fact was not lost to anthropologist Irving Goldman, when he wrote: "No part, no person, no tribe, no species, no body of super-natural beings is self-sufficient. Each possesses a portion of the sum of all the powers and properties of the cosmos; each must share with all or the entire system of nature would die. . . . Kwakiutl religion represents the concern of the people to occupy their proper place within the total system of life, and to act responsibly within it, so as to acquire and control the powers that sustain life."[1]

Thus, it is important to reflect on the genesis of the First Peoples on the Pacific Northwest Coast. This genesis is predicated on the belief of all First Nations people that the Creator brought into being the First Ancestors. Specifically, the First Ancestors evolved from and followed the creation of Heaven and Earth. According to the primal world view of our people, the definition of the world around us breaks down into four realms—the Sky World, the Undersea World, the Mortal World and the Spirit World. Ancient voices spoke of a time when the world was one, indicating absolute acknowledgment of the interconnections between those four dimensions.

THE FIRST ANCESTORS

The Kwakwaka'wakw Nation is made up of several tribes, and every tribe consists of two or more *numayms*.[2] The tribes and numayms each had a distinct First Ancestor. From a magical and supernatural transformation arose the Kwakwaka'wakw Nation. The site where each First Ancestor emerged in this world is sacred, and the locales mark the territories of the tribes. From these places of origin evolved the membership of our Nation. Over time, these progenitors created a law and an order that prevails today throughout the territory. What is remarkable is the fact that one ancient language binds our people together.

The Gwa'sala people make up one of the tribes of the Kwakwaka'wakw. It is said that their ancestors came to earth from above in a Shimmering Ray of Light. One of them came down as a brilliant event wearing the Sun mask and, upon taking it off, became a man. Another of the ancestors landed as a Whale. He came from the North End of the World and, after building a house, established one of the numayms of the tribe.[2]

The Gwawa'enuxw tribe lives in the village of Hegams, now known as Hopetown. The Gwawa'enuxw have always been taught that one of their First Ancestors was the great Thunderbird who roamed the heavens and made his home on Mount Steven. One day, in another time, he descended from the mountain. When he reached the base of the

4
Kwakw<u>aka</u>'wakw, Simon Dick
Forehead Mask Representing Wolf,
1992
60.9 × 27.0 × 23.0
red cedar, yellow cedar, horsehair, wolf fur,
styrofoam and paint
Private Collection
Photo by Trevor Mills, Vancouver Art Gallery

mountain, he shed his Thunderbird form and became one of the first human ancestors of the tribe that eventually came to occupy the village of H<u>e</u>gams.

Another story tells of two First Ancestors who founded two separate tribes, the H<u>a</u>xwa'mis and Dzawad<u>a</u>'enu<u>x</u>w, at A<del>l</del>a<del>l</del><u>x</u>u (Wakeman Sound) and Gwa'yi (Kingcome village). We are told that when daylight first came to the world, two wolves became human beings (Figure 4). One was <u>K</u>awadilik<u>a</u>la, the first Dzawad<u>a</u>'enu<u>x</u>w ancestor; the other was Kw<u>a</u>lili, the first H<u>a</u>xwa'mis ancestor. It is said that these two wolves, who were brothers, lived together for a long time at Gwa'yi, where their numbers increased. Both were shamans. One day, they were playing a game which involved throwing around a piece of quartz. <u>K</u>awadilik<u>a</u>la told his children, especially his daughter, not to look outside while the game was in progress. Unfortunately, his daughter disobeyed by peeking through a knothole in the wall of the house. This distracted <u>K</u>awadilik<u>a</u>la, who was unable to catch the quartz, which landed on a mountain now named for the crystal. He was outraged over the girl's disobedience and killed her by plucking her body into pieces. A magical and supernatural transformation took place as the torn pieces of his daughter changed into sacred eagle down. He tossed the down into the air, and it floated away. Thus it was that <u>K</u>awadilik<u>a</u>la lost the game to his younger brother Kw<u>a</u>lili.

Then the two brothers prepared for the beginning of the Great Flood by carving canoes. When the Great Flood came, they anchored themselves atop a mountain called <u>K̓</u>axwsidze', "where the waters subside." When the waters receded, the people returned to their respective territories at Wakeman Sound and Kingcome village.

These are but a very few of the First Ancestor stories that mark the time and the place of the genesis of our people. All are powerful statements about our beginnings, about our territories, about our laws, and most importantly about our kinship—how we are related. This recognition of kinship in the broadest sense reaffirms the indigenous commitment to seeking balance and harmony throughout the cosmos.

Masks have an important and significant place in our evolution. Every mask is quintessential to our desire to embrace wholeness, balance and harmony. In a simple and fundamental act of faith, we acknowledge and reaffirm our union through song and dance, ceremony and ritual.

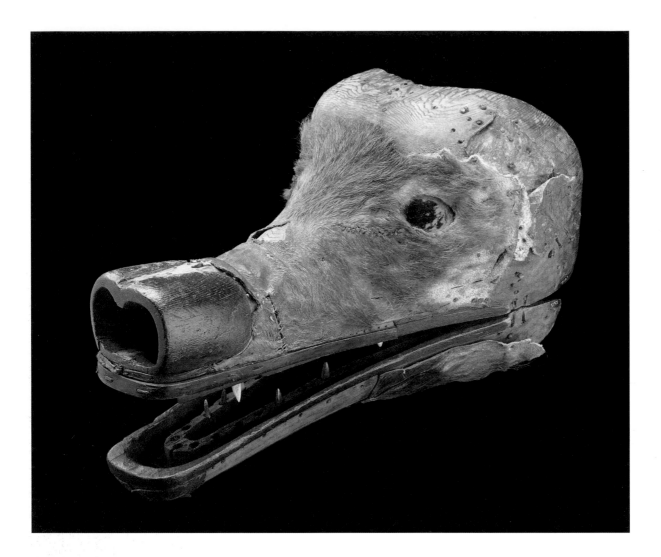

Because of our strong oral history, these matters of kinship in the immediate and broadest sense are told over and over again. They are told in family settings and recounted through song and dance. Central to this tracking of our origins is the mask. Every song and dance with a mask has a meaning that confirms and accentuates the holistic view. Generation after generation of Kwakwa̲ka'wakw people embraced the entire circle of life through the strong meaning that masks give. Through the repeated use of masks in ceremony, a reverent and spiritual appreciation has evolved to the present.

When I was a boy of about five or six years of age, I became aware of the omnipotent presence of masks. They had a life of their own—sometimes menacing and foreboding, always intrusive. Masks seemed to be everywhere. They were at home in attics and storage spaces or dancing round the fire in the Big House. Other times they would be evident round and about the village, like the Grizzly Bear (Figure 5) and Dzunuḵwa—the wild woman of the woods (Figure 6). These two really kept us kids in line. For most of us, as children in the village, it is these masks we remember the most, along with Ba̲ḵwas—the wild man of the woods and chief of the ghosts (Figure 3). We were told to behave or fall victim to the appetite of these three. Needless to say, generations of Kwakwa̲ka'wakw children behaved themselves as a result of these creatures.

5 (facing page)
Kwakw<u>aka</u>'wakw, Artist
Unknown
Mask Representing Grizzly Bear,
c. 1840
26.0 × 26.7 × 42.8
red cedar, bearskin, sinew, glass and paint
Royal British Columbia Museum, Victoria,
9187
Photo by Trevor Mills, Vancouver Art Gallery

6
Kwakw<u>aka</u>'wakw, Artist
Unknown
Mask Representing Dzunuḵwa,
late 19th century
58.0 × 42.2 × 24.0
red cedar, mirrors, fur, nails and paint
U'mista Cultural Centre, Alert Bay, 80.01.133
Photo by Trevor Mills, Vancouver Art Gallery

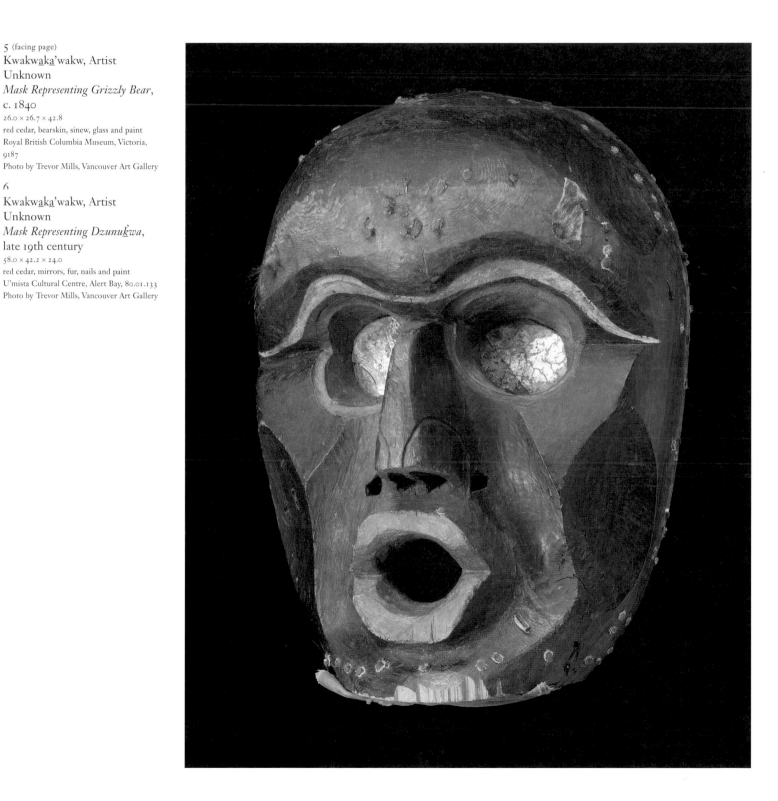

As I grew older, my apprehension about masks changed to awe and a different understanding of their significance. Each mask took on the life and spirit of the persona it represented. Dzunuḵwa took on the spirit of womanhood gone mad, one who defied the most primal maternal instinct to protect children and instead threatened them. Baḵwas was always grotesque and utterly frightening. Surely he represented the souls of men who had lost touch with reality, men who had lost sight of right and wrong, balance and harmony, men who had crossed the fine line into madness.

THE POTLATCH

In the old days, the Kwakwaka'wakw constantly sought to give meaning and purpose to their existence. As with all civilizations throughout time, they struggled to comprehend their place in the universe and were mystified by the same great riddles. So how did they define in their own human terms the wonder of the universe which is incomprehensible? They interpreted it in song and ritual, dance and ceremony, often through the use of masks.

The sum total of the Kwakwaka'wakw answer to the great mystery was and is rolled up into the Winter Ceremonies, which we call the Potlatch—a series of songs, dances and rituals. This Potlatch is the defining instrument of the great order of things past and present and yet to come.[3]

I remember the first time I danced in a mask. It was at about the same time that I first encountered Baḵwas and Dzunuḵwa. There were few white people around then. The odd logger sometimes came to our village with mad water, mad drinks. A priest might visit from time to time or even live in the village for a while. The priest said our world was wrong. Sometimes a man called Indian Agent would come. Our grandparents didn't like him much, and they were afraid of him. Other times, a policeman might arrive. Everyone scurried for cover then or peeked from behind window curtains to see what he was up to. And there were teachers and nurses, as well as doctors and missionaries. They seemed to take over all the things that the old people used to do in caring for the tribe.

The fire roared with brilliance as we prepared to dance the Atłaḵim, the dance of the Forest Spirits.[4] Excitement and mystery filled the air. I had seen this dance before, and I had seen all its masks. They were beautiful and full of life. Everyone jostled behind a great screen adorned with ancestral images. There were so many dancers, twenty or more, in various phases of readiness. People were talking to each other, getting ready, asking questions, giving instructions. Soon, everyone was fully dressed. Once inside their masks, a hush fell upon the troupe. The Forest has many voices and, sometimes, there is deafening silence; such was the moment behind the dance curtain.

As a masked dancer among the Kwakwaka'wakw, I have been in that moment countless times. It is a moment when all the world is somewhere else. I am totally and

7
Kwakwaka'wakw, Beau Dick
Mask Representing Laugher,
c. 1985
31.0 × 26.5 × 14.5
red cedar, cedar bark, nails, twine, feathers and paint
Private Collection
Photo by Trevor Mills, Vancouver Art Gallery

completely alone. My universe is the mold of the mask over my face. I am the mask. I am the bird. I am the animal. I am the fish. I am the spirit. I visualize my dance. I ponder every move. I transcend into the being of the mask. Younger dancers call it "hyping up." Suddenly, the deafening silence explodes into cacophony—birds sing, animals growl, ferns whistle in the wind. Everyone has a voice. Four times the sounds and silence collide, then the great dance begins.

Legend has it that a young boy fell out of favour with his father, the chief. Disheartened, the young boy yearned to make things right. He decided to snare a grouse for his father. Off he went deep into the forest, until he came upon a clearing. This was the place to set his snare. He set the trap and withdrew to cover. The sun shone upon the young boy and soon he fell into a deep sleep.

Magically, a tiny grouse emerged from the forest stands and then retreated. Four times it emerged from the veil, and then finally, in a complete dance around the clearing, it called the forest dominion forth in a majestic dance of life. First the Stump came to life, and then the Doorway into the Forest Spirit World. Birds were called to the dance. The souls of Skulls covered with moss joined the symphony. The animals danced, as did the fish from nearby streams. Even the Human Beings were called to join. In a glorious tribute to life, the Midwife attended a Mother who gave birth to two children (Figures 8

8
Atłakim dance staged at Gilford Village for visiting officials, 1946. The masked figure in the foreground is the Woman Giving Birth (see Figure 9), followed by the Husband and the Midwife (crouching, hands extended forward to indicate her role in the delivery). Just behind the Midwife are the Twins wearing white masks. Another child, wearing a dark mask, right hand raised, is Robert Joseph.
Photo courtesy Royal British Columbia Museum, Victoria, PN15250-3

9
Kwakw<u>a</u>ka'wakw, Willie Seaweed
*Mask Representing Woman
Giving Birth*, c. 1930
30.5 × 20.3 × 12.7
red cedar, cotton twine and paint
University of British Columbia, Museum of
Anthropology, Vancouver, A6237
Photo by Trevor Mills, Vancouver Art Gallery

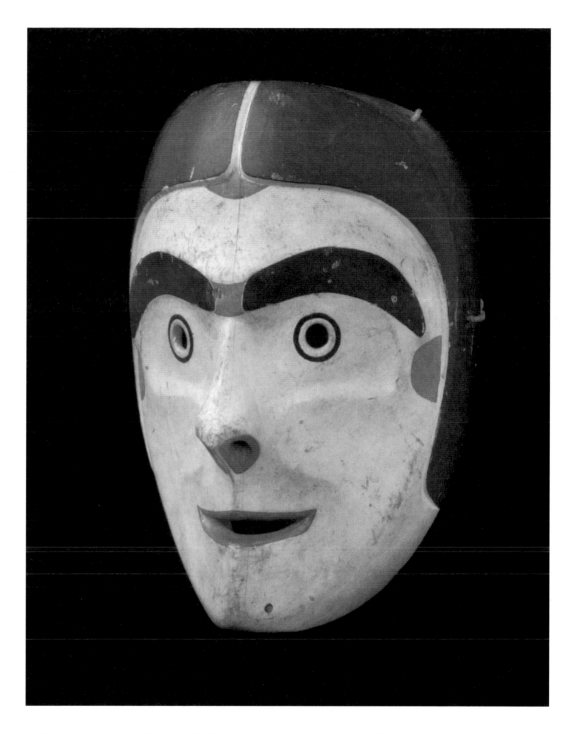

and 9). I was one of the two children in this great dance the first time I wore a mask. First, we were concealed under blankets, following the flow of dancers around the fire, always counterclockwise. We walked between the Midwife and the Mother, propelled by gentle hands, for our vision inside the mask was limited. By some ancient process, we were "born" into full view of the Big House world.

The final entity called to the dance was long-beaked Raven. From a platform high above the Big House front door, he swooped down to join the celebration of life. Grouse repeated its calls until the miracle of the tableau retreated back behind the curtain.

The chief's son woke from his deep sleep. The dream was clear in his mind. He had to tell his father about this great blessing and supernatural event that had come in a dream. Then all was well with father and son. This dance became the right of the chief and his descendants for all time.

Many years later, I discovered that the Atłakim dance belonged to one of my late uncles who acquired it through marriage. The dance originated from the Oweekeno tribe of Rivers Inlet.

THE ANTI-POTLATCH LAW

In a bid to stamp out the aboriginal people and our culture, the Canadian government enacted a law in 1884 prohibiting the Potlatch. During the Atłakim dance which I took part in and described, I remember a frightening and confusing interruption. Someone announced the arrival of unexpected visitors. Everyone scrambled from the Big House into the night.

My memory fails me somewhat, for I was then a little boy. My next recollection is that we reassembled in the Big House, still in full dress for the Atłakim, posing for pho-

tographs (Figure 10). I remember a policeman in uniform being there. No charges were laid, even though the anti-Potlatch statute was still in effect. My people were operating covertly to sustain their traditions, values and beliefs to which the mask is so integral.

The Kwakwaka'wakw were persecuted, more than any other First Nation, under this anti-Potlatch law. Chiefs and noblewomen were jailed, masks were confiscated, Big Houses were torn down, and ceremonial objects were burned. In spite of this, a higher law commanded that we continue to dance. While very few older masks and pieces of art survived in our communities, our artists came to the rescue by creating replacements that allowed us to maintain and continue our dance and ritual, primarily through the use of masks.

During this dark period of cultural repression, collectors came and pillaged many of the last remaining great objects from another time. Contemporary art became commercial art. While this was at first a glaring setback, it nevertheless was a blessing in disguise. The art form became the medium that held ceremony and ritual together while we awaited a cultural renaissance.

THE BOX OF TREASURES—THE LAW OF THE MASK

I have seen the old photographs of mounds of masks and objects that were taken from my people during the Potlatch prohibition (Figure 11). I have heard the stories about how priceless heirlooms were torched to purge our old ways. As I grew older, I remembered these stories. There have been tears even in the recalling of a time before mine.

I saw the tears again among the young and old in 1980 as we celebrated the opening of the U'mista Cultural Centre in Alert Bay. Ceremonial regalia, including dozens of masks which had been illegally acquired by the Indian Agent in 1922, was repatriated to Alert Bay from museums in eastern Canada. Our people gathered to celebrate the emotional return of the artifacts to our newly built museum. Tears flowed in joy and relief as we welcomed back ancient masks and other treasures.

Among the celebrants was Chief Tom Hunt. Midway through his speech, he broke down and wept with bittersweet tears. Tears also welled up from somewhere deep within me as I watched my great chief shudder and heave in a moment so full of emotion. A noblewoman, Agnes Cranmer, stepped in to speak for her brother.

My turn to speak would soon come up. What could I possibly say that would be more important than what this great chief had said and the feelings he had displayed? I wondered if he was thinking what I was thinking. Was it too late? Had the political and religious zealots achieved their ends? Was it over?

I stepped up to the microphone with a Sun mask tucked under my arm. I delivered words of praise to our people for this achievement of building a centre and repatriating

10 (facing page)

The Atłak̲im dance troupe at Gilford Village, 1946. The Raven mask (right) and the Huxwhukw mask (left) are in the collection of the University of British Columbia Museum of Anthropology, Vancouver. Four children associated with the Woman Giving Birth are seated in the front row. Robert Joseph is obscured by the shadow cast by the Grouse dancer.

Photo courtesy Royal British Columbia Museum, Victoria, PN15250-52

11

Masks assembled by Indian Agent William Halliday in 1922 await inventory in Alert Bay. The Dzunuk̲wa mask on the left (see Figure 6) was repatriated to the U'mista Cultural Centre in Alert Bay when it opened in 1980.

Photo courtesy Royal British Columbia Museum, Victoria, PN11636

our treasures. I spoke of victory and hope for the future. I condemned ignorance and intolerance. "It's like stripping away a man's soul," I said in reference to church and government actions aimed at destroying Indian people and our cultures. Then I presented the Sun mask to the U'mista Cultural Centre as a gesture of support and unity from the Kwagiulth Museum at Cape Mudge, which had opened a year earlier to house a part of the repatriated collection.

There are many masks in the U'mista Cultural Centre at Alert Bay and in the Kwagiulth Museum at Cape Mudge. These masks and regalia all belong to particular families. They are property. They can be owned collectively or they can be individually assigned within the family. These rights are inherent: the ownership of these masks and rights, and the entitlement to use them, must flow from previous family ownership, from generation to generation. Wider and expanding entitlement and ownership rights may spread through marriages. A dowry comes with a noble bride to acknowledge her status and to ensure that the well-being of offspring and grandchildren is secure.

It is a strict law that rules the use and display of masks and the attendant rights which reflect the full measure of a family's legacy. Masks are kept secure in special chests which we call k̕awat̕si—"boxes of treasures." When a bride brings masks as part of her dowry, they come both literally and figuratively in these prized containers. The metaphor expands when the masks are danced and the ceremonial house itself becomes a box of treasures.

MASKS OF SANCTITY

Masks have emanated through the mists of time as dreams and visions. People who have embraced them are długwala (blessed). These masks have been deemed nawalakw (supernatural). They are representations of supernatural encounters and glorious manifestations. They are a part of the Kwakwaka'wakw mind that distinguishes us from the world around us and that gives credence to our own persona. Masks have a potent and compelling force, acknowledging the need for balance and harmony. It is from this original primal view that aboriginal people recognize the entirety of the wonder. Every dancer who has danced in a mask has glimpsed this oneness.

Traditionally and ritually, masks should always be guarded, always be hidden away. Masks are never shown until they are actually danced on the floor of the ceremonial house or used in the community. It is never known which masks will be shown or which dances will take place until the event happens.

No wonder that mystery and anticipation prevail. The only people who know the order of things are the chiefs and the matriarchs. I am told that in the old days they would go deep into the woods to determine such things. When I was young, I was privy

12
Kwakwa̲ka'wakw, Artist
Unknown
Mask Representing Nuḻamaḻ,
c. 1890
46.0 × 28.0 × 23.0
red cedar, hair and paint
Royal British Columbia Museum, Victoria, 1914
Photo courtesy Royal British Columbia Museum

by chance and kinship to see such meetings. I was raised by Chief Tom Dawson, who belonged to the inner circle of chiefs and matriarchs including the likes of Chief Willie Seaweed, Chief Tom Patch Wamiss, Chief Herbert Johnson, Chief Fred Williams, Chief Tom Willie and Chief Billy Sandy Willie, just to name a few. They met in the Big House or in private homes to determine the sequence and display of masks and rights, dances and songs.

Even when masks are hidden away between use, they are carefully wrapped in sheets or blankets. If there are movable parts, these are secured or bound by strips of cedar bark or cloth. Times of least exposure, primarily the cover of darkness, are the most suitable for moving or transporting masks.

Many masks are assigned to individuals through family prerogative, and only those individuals may claim those particular masks. An example of such a mask is the Nuḻamaḻ. Literally translated, the name means "one who appears as an unwise face." This mask is characterized by an elongated nose of comic proportions (Figure 12). Paradoxically, this mask and dancer represent an important function in the dance cycle, as the Nuḻamaḻ is charged with the responsibility for maintaining protocol during potlatches. The Nuḻamaḻ dance is a contradiction of this duty. The performer appears from behind the dance curtain, screaming "Whee-ha-hee." As he circles the dance floor, he flails wildly with his arms and appears to draw mucus from his protruding nose to fling into the crowd. Was this act of wild frenzy an effort to frighten the crowd into total observance and compliance? I do not know. In 1981, during the first Potlatch I gave to assume my rank as a traditional chief, I assigned the Nuḻamaḻ dance to my youngest son. In my family, only he can dance it. Other lineages also own this dance, and it is assigned to an individual in each of these families. Other masks are collective property and can be danced by a number of people.

The most sacred of all of our dances is the H̲amsa̲mala, which means "wearing the face of the man-eating cannibal." Only Hamaṫsas, or cannibal dancers, may perform this great mask dance. The Hamaṫsa dancer and mask is the epitome of the ultimate human struggle to tame the cannibal spirit inside oneself—that spirit within that defies peace, harmony and balance. To unlock this fury is to begin to unravel the mysteries of the universe. You must go to yourself before you can go anywhere else.

There are three masks in the Hamsamala dance series, the Huxwhukw (Figure 13), the Gwa'wina (Figure 83) and the Galukwiwe' (Figure 14). It is said that these monsters, with their long and grotesque beaks shuddering and snapping with great thunder, represent the attendants of the cannibal spirit Baxwbakwalanuxwsiwe', the Cannibal-at-the-North-End-of-the-World.

Why are these magnificent and awesome celestial creatures here? They represent the final inner human conflict. The Hamatsa initiate has been to the wilderness. He has been in exile. Stark naked and utterly alone, he has descended to levels of darkness and fear hitherto unknown. He stands at the abyss of madness. Dragged to the depths of his own despair, he bottoms out and rediscovers his own humanity. Slowly, he becomes one with the wilderness around him. He becomes one with the environment, the birds and the animals. He is part of the symphony around him—of kinship and connectedness.

The next part of this great dance is the *kam'ya*, the surround and the chase, the recapturing of the Hamatsa. The initiate, clad only in hemlock branches, emerges from the cover of the forest. He is quickly corralled and ushered into the great ceremonial house. Eventually, he is adorned with rings of red cedar bark around his head, wrists, ankles and upper torso. The cedar bark represents the great life cycle and law of the Kwakwaka'wakw.

The great chiefs sing to appease the initiate. They sing of glory and praise. They sing of power and might. The cannibal spirit lingers in the body and soul of the Hamatsa initiate. Suddenly, he shrieks his terrifying cannibal scream and races around the earthen floor, finally disappearing behind the curtain—the veil between humans and the other dimensions.

The snapping of giant carnivorous beaks breaks the deafening silence, and the face of the cannibal, the spirit of the cannibal, comes to dance for the last time. The giant celestial beings appear one at a time, and four times the initiate is pulled between chaos and order. Terror finally exits as the Hamsamala ends.

The Hamsamala is the most protected of all Kwakwaka'wakw masked dances. It has to be performed by trained, initiated dancers, and it has to be done right. There is no room for error, for there is no room for chaos and terror.

The speaker of the house chants a sacred song and acknowledges the entirety of the universe by saluting the four directions. "All has gone well," he says, "we have once again mastered this ritual that our ancestors embraced with sanctity and greatness."

A general and common world view held by Native people is that all things are linked together. This interrelationship demands that a certain level of balance and harmony be sustained to ensure survival in the broadest sense. Many legends and masks

13
Kwakwaka'wakw, Doug Cranmer
Mask Representing Huxwhukw,
1971
27.4 × 26.0 × 180.0
red cedar, cedar bark, leather, nails, twine and
paint
Royal British Columbia Museum, Victoria, 13948
Photo courtesy Royal British Columbia Museum

14
Kwakwaka'wakw, Willie Seaweed
Mask Representing Crooked-Beak,
c. 1954
73.6 × 30.5 × 106.7
red cedar, wood, cedar bark, cotton twine,
nails and paint
University of British Columbia, Museum of
Anthropology, Vancouver, A8327
Photo by Bill Holm

speak to this principle. A mask in dance can acknowledge this obligation to the wholeness of the world view.

Other masks include those that represent First Ancestors. The previously mentioned wolf ancestor and Thunderbird, as well as the whale, are included in this category. All the members of a numaym are entitled to use masks of its First Ancestor. Those who are not members of the numaym are forbidden to use them.

The mask called Imas represents the return of a loved one from the spirit world—from the dead. He or she may be someone who passed away recently. This person may have been high-ranking and heavily laden with rights and privileges. The Imas returns wearing a sacred cedar bark ring around his or her neck, escorted by noble chiefs chanting as the drummers and singers tap quietly and gently on logs and drums so as to give suasion and movement to the spirit visitor. After slowly emerging from the front entrance of the Big House and circling around the fire, the Imas exits at the same point that it entered.

The noble chiefs return with sacred cedar bark in hand. The speaker shouts with jubilation, announcing that the sacred cedar bark has been returned after all and that it has not been lost to the spirit world. This is a great dance that symbolizes the continuing transference of a living culture. This is a dance that acknowledges the complete cycle and continuity of life. Not all families may conduct this ceremony, so only a select few may use this mask.

Several dances recount the adventures of an ancestral hero who encounters an array of creatures; more than twenty and as many as forty different masks may be used in these series. Because these dances are so spectacular and entertaining, there is considerable pressure for collective presentations of them, even if the right properly belongs to an individual or a numaym. The previously mentioned Atłakim is an example. The Animal Kingdom dance of the Kwikwasutinuxw tribe and the Undersea Realm dance of the Gwawa'enuxw tribe also require a family affiliation as a prerequisite for participation. There always are lead or star dancers of these groups. Many dancers audition to fill these roles and practices are held behind closed doors.

I remember auditions and practices for the Grouse caller and the Stump dancer at Kingcome village when I was young. Chiefs Jim Dick and Tom Patch Wamiss always seemed to have the role of selecting dancers. I was about fourteen years old. I donned the mask, took a deep breath and waited for my cue. The pounding beat on a hollow log drum rattled, and I jumped into action. As I sprang into full view, I became disoriented, causing roars of laughter. One by one, other aspirants fell to the same fate; they also faced laughter and friendly ridicule. Charlie Dick and Dan Willie retained their positions as chosen dancers that day; we were no threat to them. The same process of audition and practice took place for the Hamsamala dancers as well.

The longest performance that I took part in was as the Kingfisher in the Animal Kingdom dance of the K̲wik̲wasutinux̲w. This drama has a format similar to the Atłak̓im, in that the Wolf and the Kingfisher spend the duration of the event repeatedly calling forth all manner of beasts. Much thought, much preparation, went into this dance. First, the masks were laid out by a person designated as the caretaker and custodian of the secret place behind the dance curtain. It was off limits for others so that the mystique was maintained. It was also guarded so that no one could tamper with the paraphernalia. Everything was checked for comfort and working order. Then the masks were handed to the dancers. Great care was given to fitting the costumes and masks by the custodian and designated helpers.

Each dancer who was to appear reflected on his or her own dance and the character to be portrayed. There were questions and there were instructions in a room tense with anticipation. Soon, everyone was lined up in the order that they would appear in this extraordinary dance. Inevitably, a silence would descend upon the troupe as each dancer considered his or her own thoughts under the concealment of the mask. They were ready. They were the Animal Kingdom.

I was good at this dance. I imagined the Kingfisher and I was the Kingfisher. I jumped and I swooped, I dived, full of exhilaration. I felt a surge of power and dominion over the animal world that came forth at my beckoning. Finally, I called the dancers back behind the veil.

THE POWERS OF MASKS

During preparations for my first Potlatch at Gilford village, I did some research into my family background and met an elder who informed me that my grandmother had been initiated as a ghost dancer in the 1930s. She had a Skull headpiece that she wore perched atop her head and concealed her face with hemlock boughs when she danced.

The elder entrusted the headpiece to a relative until it could be presented to its rightful owner. At the time, the relative's family lived at Cape Mudge village on Quadra Island. They were haunted by ghostly apparitions and frightening and unexplainable sounds, they said. Eventually, they moved to a new home on the Quinsam Reserve at Campbell River. In the Indian world, for the most part, new houses are never haunted. But to the family's dismay, they discovered that whatever was haunting them had followed them to their new home. Small men were sighted by more than one member of the family, doors opened and shut by themselves, and they heard noises when there was no one around. The family lived in a two-storey home with a flight of stairs leading to the front entrance. A platform level divided the stairway from the top floor to the downstairs front entrance. One day, a family member fell and broke her leg there. In that

NOTES

I
Irving Goldman, *The Mouth of Heaven: An Introduction to Kwakiutl Religious Thought*, 177.

2
In his various writings, anthropologist Franz Boas used the term "tribe" to distinguish the twenty independent village groups of the Kwakiutl (or Kwakwaka̱'wakw as they are now known). Each tribe consisted of two to seven closely related social units called *'na̱'mima* (one kind), anglicized to the spelling *numaym* in the anthropological literature. Every tribe and each numaym had a distinct First Ancestor, whose image was represented on totem poles, house frontal paintings, dance blankets, settees and other ceremonial gear, including masks.

3
The format and concept of the Potlatch varies from one Northwest Coast Nation to another. Essential to all, however, is a public display of privileges presented as songs, names, titles, dances and masks that confirm the ancient (mythic and real) histories of a chiefly lineage. Invited guests who witness the oratorical and theatrical presentations are feasted and ultimately paid by the host group. By accepting material and monetary gifts, the witnesses publicly validate and confirm their host's claim to the displayed entitlements.

4
For a full account of the Atła̱kim dance, see Franz Boas, *Ethnology of the Kwakiutl*, 1179-220. Briefly, a young man who is ill-treated by his father leaves his village and follows a nearby river to its source. Arriving at a supernatural place, he bathes ritually for four days. Each night, a visitor appears and predicts that the boy will be granted a great treasure in the form of a dance. Eventually, the boy is led into the realm of the Forest Spirits through a doorway revealed when a carpet of moss is pulled back from the forest floor. A Grouse calls a succession of creatures, including cannibal birds, a personified Door, a Stump on which the Grouse danced in a vision revealed to hero before he entered the house of the Forest Spirits, a Midwife who attends a Woman Giving Birth to twins, a Salmon Spirit, a Laugher (Figure 7) and others. Finally, the young man returns triumphant to his mother's village where he makes public his hard-won treasure.

instant, the Skull headpiece, which was stored beneath that platform, came to mind. To try to quell the spirits, they burned incense, they burned cedar boughs, they called in a local priest. Nothing worked.

By the time I showed up at their front door to inquire about the Skull headpiece, the family were more than happy to turn it over to me. After telling me about its eventful history, they urged me to take it away.

I took the piece to my home that night, carefully concealed in a box, and placed it in the basement. My second-oldest son, who slept in the basement, knew nothing about this. The first night was uneventful, but during the second night, he suddenly awoke from a deep sleep and was gripped with utter terror. Ashen faced, he raced upstairs and roused my wife and me. Trembling, he told us of this experience, which he said was accompanied by flashes of brilliant rays of light. My wife, who knew about the headpiece and its history, demanded that I "get the thing out of the house." Just prior to all this, I had been awakened by a gentle tug on our blankets. At first, I had thought it might be one of our small children or maybe just a dream. Could the two incidents have been related?

Slowly, I dressed, retrieved the box with the Skull headpiece and carried it to my car. I thought immediately of using one of the outside lockers at the local bus depot. It was spooky driving there. The box stayed in a locker for a couple of days while I looked for a new home for the Skull. Luckily, the staff of the local museum in Campbell River agreed to look after it for a while. Now, my oldest son, who lives in Vancouver, keeps the headpiece. No events have ever taken place at his home.

Have we become too far removed from the earth and the four dimensions to relate to the supernatural and to the inherent powers of masks? I do not know.

POWER OF THE SHINING HEAVENS

PETER MACNAIR

FOR MILLENNIA, the indigenous peoples of the Pacific Northwest Coast of North America have produced a wondrous array of masks; those featured here were made from the 1790s up to today. To appreciate the meaning of these masks, we must define them in form and time, as well as in terms of their context. While we can bring our Western concepts of art, often distilled to the rubric of connoisseurship, to the artifact, understanding it from the point of view of both the maker and the user will greatly enrich our experience of it. To celebrate the object only for its aesthetic is to create an icon bereft of meaning; once meaning and context are lost, value is forever diminished.

The First Nations that occupy the Northwest Coast, from the Strait of Juan de Fuca north to Yakutat Bay, speak several disparate languages, but they display ceremonial, technological and economic similarities, and they can be considered to share definitive cultural elements. An institution fundamental to the more than a dozen tribal groups that inhabit this vast littoral is the Potlatch which unifies them in both a physical and intellectual sense. All aspects of their culture—language, polity, economics, land tenure, belief, ritual and art—are inextricably bound up in the complex Potlatch system. When civil and religious authorities in Canada and the United States sought to eradicate the Potlatch in the final quarter of the nineteenth century, they attacked the rationale for existence of a people whose sophisticated culture had been evolving for millennia.

Central to the Potlatch, and thus the entire culture, is the need to protect, maintain and transfer privileges that go back to the beginning of time, when magic ancestors changed at will from supernatural to human form at specific geographic sites along the coastal waterways and rivers. These locales came to designate the territorial boundaries that today define the homelands of more than one hundred independent village groups.

Images of these primal ancestors, be they creatures of the Sky, Mortal, Sea or Spirit World, were displayed in powerful sculptural or painted icons displayed on housefront paintings, storage chests, utensils, totem poles and other monumental carvings, dance blankets, ceremonial regalia, and masks. These images are called crests, and they serve to identify the Bears, Killer Whales, Eagles, Ravens, Wolves, Thunderbirds and other beings from which the various family groups descended.

One dramatic way of recreating the magical past is through the use of masks in elaborately staged theatrical events performed for a sophisticated audience which is willing to suspend disbelief as birds transform into serpents, wolves into killer whales, celestial objects into humans. The mask comes alive when worn by a skilled dancer and animated through movement, especially in front of a fire whose flames highlight and soften the sculptural planes of the mask as it moves from light through shadow to light again.

While dance presentations are deliberately crafted to impress, the purpose of the performance is to validate the ancient and honourable history of the mask owner's family. Attendant songs are sung, detailed family chronicles are retold; particular names and the

15
Haida, Kaigani Haida Artist
Mask Representing Djilakons, before 1828
25.4 × 19.1 × 9.7
wood and paint
Peabody Essex Museum, Salem, E3483
Photo by Mark Sexton, courtesy Peabody Essex Museum

right to ceremonial positions accompany the mask and are as much a part of the legacy as is the tangible object itself. Together, all of these prerogatives are inalienable. The owner must maintain the privilege through public display and payment to designated witnesses of the performance. If the host satisfies his guests with his authority and largesse, he will, in time, be able to transfer the privilege to an appropriate successor.

THE FORMS OF NORTHWEST COAST ART

The art of the Northwest Coast is highly developed sculpturally and graphically, and frequently both are combined in ways which celebrate the intellectual capacity and achievement of this unique art form. A number of subtle differences characterize regional, tribal, local and personal styles, and these distinctions are easily observed in masks. Described below are a select few that can be considered classic examples; their distinguishing features provide a basis for comparison with and understanding of other works.

Many of the masks illustrated here represent the human face or some anthropomorphic rendering of an animal or supernatural being. The Tlingit mask featured in Figure 16 is obviously intended to depict a person, but the anatomical proportions are far from those of the human visage. On the mask, the forehead is truncated, the eyebrows are massive and dominant, the eye sockets curve uncharacteristically from under brow to upper lip, and the broad mouth with wide flat lips is more stylized than realistic. An examination of the Tlingit masks illustrated in Figures 17 and 18 determines that these traits are consistent within the group's style and remain so even when a birdlike creature is depicted (Figure 152).

Strikingly different is the style found in the work of artists from among the Tsimshian Peoples: the Nisg̲a'a, Git̲xsan, Coast Tsimshian and Southern Tsimshian.[1] The Nisg̲a'a mask representing a personified Moon tends towards naturalism in form (Figure 1), and the relationship between skin, muscle and bone is much more evident than in the Tlingit examples. In the Nisg̲a'a mask, a soft three-sided pyramid defines the cheek; the eyes are proportionally much smaller and the stylized eyebrows are more restrained than in Tlingit works. The treatment of the facial features is similar in the Nisg̲a'a conceited woman mask (Figure 20). A Git̲xsan variant appears in the spirit mask illustrated in Figure 19; the overall proportions differ slightly, but the underlying structural similarity between this one and the two Nisg̲a'a works is clear. This consistency in the treatment of anatomical elements within a group's style helps to attribute undocumented or questionably recorded examples such as the Moon mask in Figure 21; it is obviously Tsimshian in style, although to date it has been thought to be Haida.

Admittedly, Haida masks sometimes are difficult to identify: like the Nisg̲a'a and Git̲xsan examples, they tend towards a realistic representation of the human face. Certain

17
Tlingit, Artist Unknown
Mask, c. 1850
31.7 × 48.2 × 52.0
wood, pigment and hide
American Museum of Natural History, New
York, 16.1/996
Photo by Trevor Mills, Vancouver Art Gallery

16
Tlingit, Artist Unknown
Mask Representing Human Face,
c. 1850, collected before 1867
22.2 × 20.3 × 11.4
alder, hide and paint
Seattle Art Museum, Gift of John H.
Hauberg, Seattle, 91.1.118
Photo by Paul Macapia, courtesy Seattle
Art Museum

18 (facing page)
Tlingit, Artist Unknown
Headdress Mask, c. 1850
22.8 × 27.9 × 34.2
wood, pigment, abalone shell and metal
American Museum of Natural History, New
York, 19/918
Photo by Trevor Mills, Vancouver Art Gallery

19
Gitxsan, Artist Unknown
*Naxnóx Mask Representing
Human*, 19th century
22.0 × 20.8 × 11.3
wood and paint
McMichael Canadian Art Collection,
Kleinburg, 1969.28
Photo by Trevor Mills, Vancouver Art Gallery

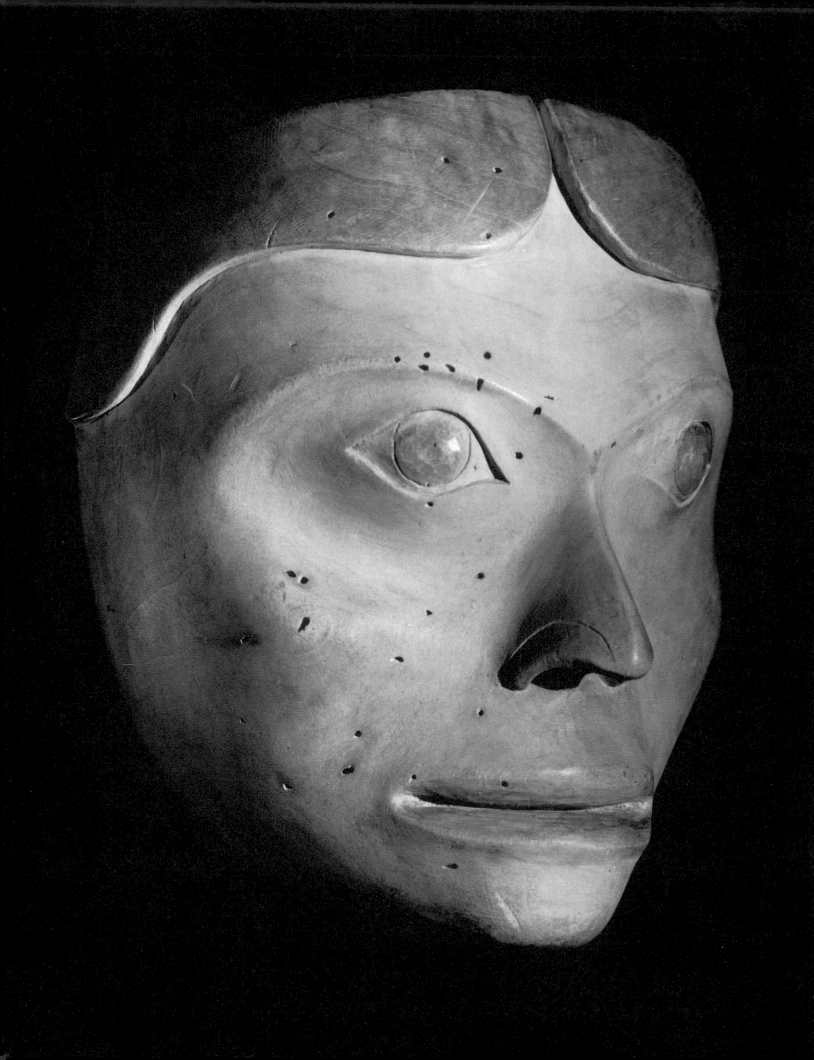

subschools within the Haida tradition are well documented and are an aid to attribution, but other examples are more problematic. The two-dimensional painted designs applied to the masks in Figures 15 and 38 are conceptually and structurally similar to those in Figure 66, supporting its Haida attribution.

Certain masks collected in the mid-nineteenth century from Heiltsuk territory fall into a distinctive substyle, but by no means have all the variants been identified. A characteristic type is the central face in Figure 22B, which is revealed when the bird in Figure 22A transforms. While its anatomical features are somewhat stylized, the proportions of the inner face are largely naturalistic. The eye socket is leaf-shaped, a form that is repeated in the eyeball itself. The application of two-dimensional design is masterful: solid blue-green U-shaped forms are painted across the forehead, the temples and the cheeks. The eye sockets are emphasized by a thin outline in red. Overlapping two-dimensional designs, in both red and black, combine to create a corona which surrounds the central face. These painted designs are so abstract that it is impossible to interpret them.

The close connection between Heiltsuk and Nuxalk styles becomes evident when the masks shown in Figures 22B and 74B are compared. Although the conceptual, temporal and spatial similarities are obvious, the faces differ significantly. The Nuxalk mask (Figure 74B) has more bulbous cheeks, created by an undercut which follows the lower eyebrow out to the temple; the eye sockets are higher and less open, the nose is heavier, and the mouth somewhat more compressed. Superimposing this face upon the Nuxalk mask in Figure 60 reveals that nearly all the sculptural planes of both align. The visage of the Sun mask in Figure 23 fits in a similar manner, supporting a Nuxalk attribution rather than the long-standing Haida one.

The term "old Wakashan" is used to describe the archaic sculptural style shared long ago by the Nuu-chah-nulth and Kwakwa̱ka'wakw peoples, but which evolved differently in the two groups. Early in the historic period, the Kwakwa̱ka'wakw style began to incorporate minimal but wholly integrated painted design elements to considerable effect (Figure 24). Using a curved knife blade, the artist made a series of parallel grooves to create an impression of fur covering the entire head of this Wolf. The majority of such pieces come from the Quatsino Sound area on northern Vancouver Island, and nearly all

22A
Heiltsuk*, Artist Unknown
(closed view)
Transformation Mask, c. 1865
33.0 × 38.0 × 68.5
wood, hair, leather and paint
Canadian Museum of Civilization, Hull,
VII-B-20
Photo courtesy Canadian Museum of
Civilization, s86-386

22B (facing page)
Heiltsuk*, Artist Unknown
(open view)
Transformation Mask, c. 1865
wood, hair, leather and paint
Canadian Museum of Civilization, Hull,
VII-B-20
Photo courtesy Canadian Museum of
Civilization, s86-387

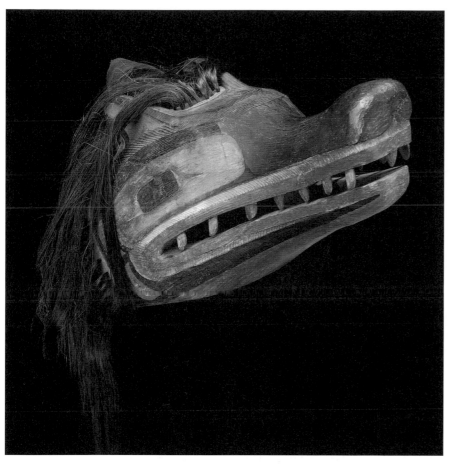

23 (facng page)
Nuxalk*, Artist Unknown
Mask Representing Sun, c. 1870
39.0 × 35.0
wood and paint
Canadian Museum of Civilization, Hull,
VII-B-19
Photo courtesy Canadian Museum of
Civilization, S92-4170

24
Kwakwaka'wakw, Artist
Unknown
Forehead Mask Representing Wolf,
c. 1840
55.8 × 55.8 × 83.8
wood, pigment and hair
American Museum of Natural History, New
York, 16/8200
Photo by Trevor Mills, Vancouver Art Gallery

represent Wolves. A subtype emerged from this distinctive school by the mid-nineteenth century, represented by the Kwakwaka'wakw Wolf masks shown in Figures 125 and 126. Eyebrows, eye sockets and nostrils are first defined by lightly engraved lines, then painted white; most of the remaining ground is covered with lustrous black graphite. Lips and nostrils may be highlighted with a brilliant vermilion, a pigment introduced by maritime fur traders.

The presence from 1833 to 1843 of the Hudson's Bay Company's Fort McLoughlin in Heiltsuk territory played a role in the development of tribal styles, because peoples from all over the coast were drawn to this trading centre. As the various groups mixed together, they adopted, adapted and appropriated artistic ideas from one another. By 1850, the Kwakwaka'wakw had assumed a number of Heiltsuk rituals, acquired either by marriage or through warfare. Some Kwakwaka'wakw masks reflect the old Wakashan sculptural form overlaid by Heiltsuk graphic elements, as the design surrounding the face of the Sun mask in Figure 25 indicates. By 1900, sculptural changes also had evolved and become standardized, including a rectangular eye socket and a flat, horizontal cheek plane (Figures 26, 67, 68, 82, 106, and 116).

In contrast to the Kwakwaka'wakw style, Nuu-chah-nulth masks collected in the eighteenth century display a flat, frontal alignment and are minimally decorated, if at all (Figures 27 and 31). By 1860, they had become triangular in cross-section and were increasingly decorated with geometric designs (Figures 28 and 58). By 1950, only vestiges of these forms survived, but contemporary artists such as Joe David (Figure 29), Ron Hamilton (Figure 141) and Art Thompson (Figures 77 and 139) have successfully reintroduced them. Tim Paul recently returned to the ancient format (Figure 30), although his applied design has a contemporary narrative function. His mask represents a November Moon; the beginning of that month is indicated by the crescent rendered in low relief across the forehead. Its profile stands out against a sky filled with snowflakes which anticipate the winter season. These waft down each temple and stars emblazon each cheek.

Speakers of the many coastal languages assert that there is no word in their nomenclature for art and that, by implication, the concept is an alien one. This is a difficult gap to bridge, especially when many contemporary Northwest Coast artists are

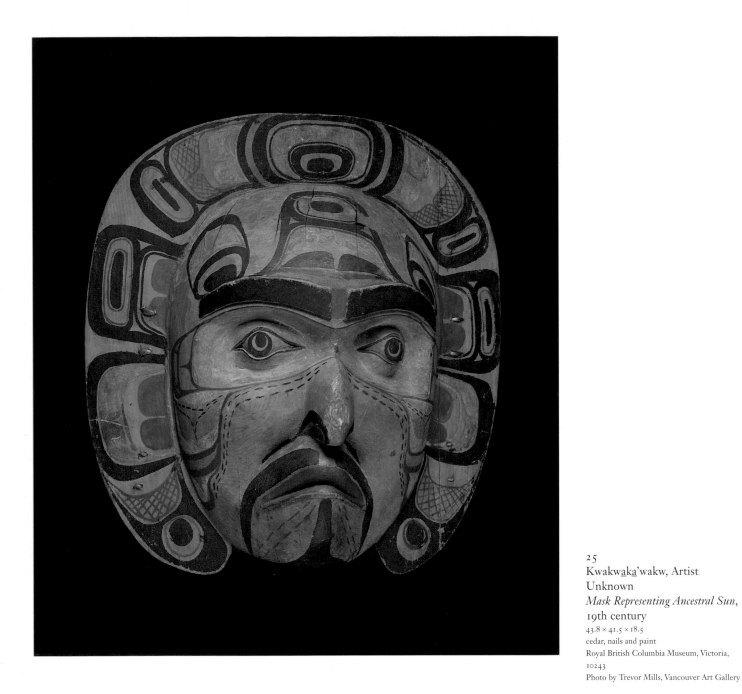

25
Kwakw<u>aka</u>'wakw, Artist
Unknown
Mask Representing Ancestral Sun,
19th century
43.8 × 41.5 × 18.5
cedar, nails and paint
Royal British Columbia Museum, Victoria,
10243
Photo by Trevor Mills, Vancouver Art Gallery

26 (facing page)
Kwakw<u>aka</u>'wakw, Charlie James*
(open view) *Transformation Mask
Representing Ancestral Sun,*
c. 1910
75.0 × 67.0 × 35.0
red cedar, cotton twine, leather, nails and paint
Royal British Columbia Museum, Victoria,
1908
Photo by Trevor Mills, Vancouver Art Gallery

27
Nuu-chah-nulth, Artist
Unknown
Mask Representing Male Ancestor,
18th century
20.7 × 17.3 × 12.5
wood and paint
Museum für Völkerkunde, Vienna, 293
Photo courtesy Museum für Völkerkunde

28
Nuu-chah-nulth, Artist
Unknown
Mask Representing Male Ancestor,
c. 1870
36.7 × 32.5 × 27.6
wood and paint
Canadian Museum of Civilization, Hull,
VII-F-385
Photo courtesy Canadian Museum of
Civilization, 72-6839

29
Nuu-chah-nulth, Joe David
Mask Representing Ancestor, 1976
27.9 × 18.0 × 17.7
red cedar and paint
Royal British Columbia Museum, Victoria,
14981
Photo by Trevor Mills, Vancouver Art Gallery

30
Nuu-chah-nulth, Tim Paul
Mask Representing November Moon, 1996
54.0 × 49.0 × 22.0
red cedar and paint
Collection of Dr. C. Schulz and Dr. J. Striegel
Photo by Trevor Mills, Vancouver Art Gallery

negotiating to have their work accepted into galleries and museums. Although it may be true there is no equivalent term for "art," the concept of aesthetics is clearly well established. The unquestionable fact is that a system of aesthetics guided both the sculptor and the painter in the Northwest Coast tradition and was clearly vested in a set of rules, which artists mastered through an apprenticeship.

The late 'Nak̓waxda'x̱w artist Charlie George once described the procedures employed in measuring out the proportions and making the sequential cuts on a block of wood from the moment the mask was conceived through its completion. All of these steps were defined by specific terms, indicating that the entire process had been intellectualized and systematized.[2] Anthropologist Samuel A. Barrett recorded more than two dozen Kwak̓wala language terms for elements of masks and dance costumes.[3] A careful reading of his list reveals these are more than just anatomical terms and are in fact instructions to the artist.

Once the rules and conventions of a given tradition or style have been mastered, an accomplished carver can produce a more than acceptable work with relative ease. His genius can bring life to almost any object, even if the detail, symmetry and proportion are not quite as accomplished as the critic might demand. In the old days, many ceremonial objects—such as shaman's charms and raven rattles—were so small that only an elite few could get close enough to them to appreciate their accomplished form. In any case, what is important is not the objects but what the objects represent: they are metaphors for ritual power or chiefly authority, and the refinements of physical appearance are not always apparent to an assembled throng.

In a sense, the same applies to masks. Often viewed in shadowed, flickering firelight and rarely in an arrested pose, masks invoke the image of an ancestor, the terror of a monster, the serenity of a celestial orb. The debate on whether or not such works are "art" obscures their meaning and intent. For anyone outside the culture, it is impossible to fully understand the relationship between mythic history as manifest in the mask and its animated presence on the stage of a ceremonial house when a skilled dancer brings life to the mask.

COMMERCE ON THE COAST

The Russian, Spanish, British and French explorers who visited the north Pacific Ocean in the late eighteenth century inevitably came into contact with the indigenous peoples who lived on the Northwest Coast. The earliest voyages were journeys of discovery driven by a scientific, intellectual and commercial curiosity about regions hitherto unknown to Europeans. Vitus Bering, Juan Pérez, James Cook, Juan Francisco de la Bodega y Quadra, George Vancouver, Alejandro Malaspina, Dioniso Alcalá Galiano, Jean François

Galaup de la Pérouse and other explorers were charged with charting the wilderness waterways and assessing the economic potential of the north Pacific. Their patrons were particularly interested in the geography, natural history and occupants of these new lands. Official artists, naturalists and observers assigned to the expeditions recorded, in meticulous detail, the flora and fauna of this remote region; they also devoted considerable effort to describing and illustrating the lives and customs of the occupants of the land through diaries, portraiture and landscapes.

While the onsite sketches and journal descriptions confirmed the lifestyle of "exotic" peoples, the artifacts or "artificial curiosities" provided evidence of ways of life almost inconceivable to the European mind. Tools, weapons, utensils, clothing and, importantly, ceremonial objects (Figures 27 and 31) acquired during these early expeditions were eventually placed in public collections.[4] As their journals reveal, many explorers marvelled at the architecture, watercraft and monumental artifacts they were privileged to view. Their positive response is a result of experiencing the objects in their proper setting. In many instances, the integrity of the artifacts was demeaned once they were deposited in European collections remote from their context, as this 1803 description of artifacts collected by Captain James Cook and accessioned into the British Museum collection reveals: "The genius of these savages may be pronounced truly original; and this is evinced by their carvings of heads and figures on the Western coast of America, from California Northward. These can hardly be said to resemble the human face divine. They are marked by the most shocking disproportion of features, and the heads have tufts of coarse hair fastened on them, with the teeth of animals set between the lips."[5]

The intrepid English explorer Captain James Cook charted the Northwest Coast in 1778. Following his violent and untimely death on a side trip to the Sandwich (Hawaiian) Islands, the expedition returned to the Northwest Coast, where some sailors happened to trade with the inhabitants for sea otter pelts. When the ships put into Canton, China, an international port of trade, the crewmen discovered, to their astonishment, that a single sea otter pelt had a value of one hundred American dollars.

This event had a profound effect on the lives of Northwest Coast peoples. Over millennia, their world had undergone a slow, predictable evolution and acculturation, but with the arrival of European and American fur traders late in the eighteenth century, communication and social intercourse among native groups expanded greatly. This soon led to the emergence of powerful chiefly dynasties such as those of Maquinna, Cuneah, Sebassa, Legaik, Shakes and Boston to name only a few. We can but marvel at the extent of their influence and fame, enhanced through their control of the fur trade which also made them wealthy. These chiefly names, which first appear in the late eighteenth century ships' journals, were handed on down through the generations and continued to occur in Hudson's Bay Company records until the mid-nineteenth century. Through surviving

31
Nuu-chah-nulth, Artist
Unknown
*Mask Representing Spirit
Ancestor*, 18th Century
28.0 × 22.0 × 15.0
wood and paint
Bernisches Historisches Museum, Bern, A1.13
Photo by Stefan Rebsamen, courtesy
Bernisches Historisches Museum

oral traditions, the histories of these chiefs still play a large role in the anthropological texts of the twentieth century.

The often uneasy alliances between great chiefs were cemented through marriage, with the attendant exchange of property and privileges in the form of titles, names, songs and, significantly, ceremonial objects and regalia. Many of the rituals now practised by peoples from northern Vancouver Island to southeast Alaska originated on the central coast among the Heiltsuk; their dissemination was accelerated by the social and artistic fervour resulting from the new wealth.

Chiefly rivalries in acquiring and displaying privileges and wealth were very public acts, expressed through the medium of the Potlatch. Chiefs travelled widely along the coast, displaying their ceremonial finery on countless occasions and at numerous venues. Among their retainers were the artists who produced the frontlets, rattles, blankets and masks that are the symbols of chiefly office. The expanded opportunity to communicate and create major works accelerated the evolution of subject and form throughout the nineteenth century.

The ceremonial artifacts acquired by the expeditions of discovery in the late eighteenth and early nineteenth centuries are true ethnographic specimens, which only their noble owners would have had the power to trade away. With increasing contact with both neighbouring tribes and foreigners came an emancipation which allowed artisans to market a product independent of their masters. This is especially evident in the Haida tradition of carving argillite, a soft black stone. From its inception in the 1820s, argillite carving—which took the form of model poles and houses, platters and pipes—was an art produced exclusively for sale. The stylistic range evident in early examples demonstrates that many practitioners quickly entered the trade.

Parallel to the genesis of argillite carving is the making of masks for sale. We can only speculate as to how and why an artist first defied his patron's authority by producing a work for trade to a Boston man (American) or a King George man (British). Quite possibly the creator was also a person of high rank and thus had the power to initiate such a departure from the norm; certainly many late nineteenth- and early twentieth-century artists were chiefs.

An examination of surviving commercial masks reveals that these were first made in the 1820s by Haida artists. These works have all the characteristics of a ceremonial piece, with the exception of rigging for wearing the mask, such as a bite piece which the wearer would grip in his teeth (Figure 32), or an inset which would allow the wearer to hold the mask, or some kind of harness which would secure it to the wearer's head. Also, there is no indication of wear other than museum neglect, so we must conclude they represent the beginning of a new commercial mask-making tradition. Insofar as we cannot name these early artists, they are anonymous. But there is no anonymity in creative genius. Nuances of design and form became trademarks, insinuating their brilliance through the decades, allowing us to attribute works to schools or unnamed but individual artists.

After the publication of Cook's journals, a group of Boston entrepreneurs recognized the potential of the trade in sea otter pelts and mounted the first American trading expedition to the Northwest Coast in 1785. For most of the next fifty years, the Americans and British dominated the sea otter trade, which ended only with the near-extinction of the animal in the north Pacific. This second wave of adventurers to the coast continued the interest in acquiring artificial curiosities made by the indigenous inhabitants. The Americans took a systematic approach to recording ethnographic objects acquired through their trading ventures. As an example, the East India Marine Society was established in 1799 in Salem, Massachusetts, "to collect and exhibit objects of interest that illuminated their voyages around the world."[6] The objects they acquired on the Northwest Coast are seminal to our study.

As the sea otter population declined, it was replaced by the land-based fur trade. In 1821, the Hudson's Bay Company began to set up trading posts along the Northwest Coast.

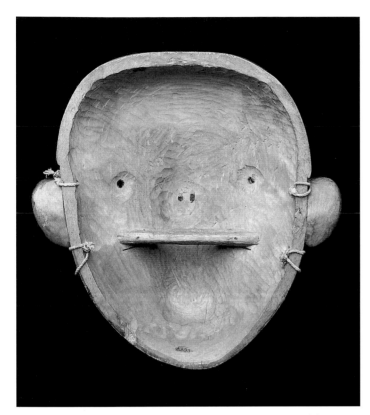

32
Detail of the inside of a mask
(Figure 52), showing the bite
piece which the dancer grips
between his teeth.
Photo by Trevor Mills, Vancouver Art Gallery

Both the Company and its senior employees independently encouraged the acquisition of ethnographic specimens for the private collections of patrons and museums in Britain.

The journal of William Fraser Tolmie, a trader and physician with the Hudson's Bay Company, bears this out. In 1838, he dispatched a box of biological specimens and artifacts to the Inverness Museum in Scotland, including "Masks used by the Indians on the Northwest Coast at their winter feasts & dances." A year later, he sent vocabularies for seventeen Native American languages, crania and a "NWC Mask" to a colleague in Paris.[8]

On November 27, 1834, Tolmie attended a Potlatch at a Heiltsuk village, and his description of the event is one of the most complete and perceptive for its time. He immediately understood he was witnessing a major event and was quick to see it in technical theatre terms. For example, he refers to the sacred room behind the painted dance screen, accessible only to chiefs and designated performers, as the "Green Room." The sensitivity and clarity of his reportage is equal to that recorded by anthropologists of a later century and deserves to be quoted at some length:

A wall of painted boards reaching from the floor to the level of eaves extending from side to side & having a small door way in centre, formed a screen behind which the actors & artists prepared for the evening's entertainment. Was introduced into this Sanctum Sanctorum . . . [which contained] . . . an immense chest of foreign manufacture containing masks. In the centre of the room glimmered a small fire & on the back wall of house there was a doorway communicating externally. Seated around the fire with brush & pallet were several artists giving the finishing stroke to the masks—others were daubing their faces with paint, which they applied by means of a small leathern bag everted. Others again were in the hands of Peruquiers whose office it was to adorn the well greased hair of their customers with down. . . . While the inmates of the Green Room were thus employed in the outer apartment, a large fire had been kindled around which the savages were singing & dancing. All the masks were representations of the "human face divine" except one which resembled that of the Falco Leucocephalus [bald eagle] & beset with the tail feathers of that bird radiating from its edge all around—it was called Tech te cheinny & seemed to be held in great reverence . . . by pulling a string which the wearer can do with his mouth, two pieces of shining brass are made to pass from within over the eye, like the film of a bird's eye—a rude wooden horn was occasionally blown & was believed without to be the voice of the Tech-te-cheinny. Common masks called Nawilock, other articles of dress displayed were blankets made from the wool of the Mountain Goat of a pretty pattern—colours black and yellow. . . .

The master of ceremonies . . . then steps forth & calls on the spirit of a chief deceased this summer to appear—the voice of Tech te cheinny is heard & presently a figure dressed in a native blanket kilt & leggings & with the Teghtecheinny mask issues & slowly makes a circuit of the apartment being preceded by a man rattling a small box containing stones & followed by another blowing down on his head, he then retires.[9]

Tolmie's observation that artists are still painting details on masks just prior to the performance is interesting. Contemporary Northwest Coast artists will appreciate that their forebears were as pressured then as they sometimes are today to finish a piece for a Potlatch. (In fact, an important tool in the modern mask maker's kit is a hair dryer to hasten the drying of acrylic paint.) Tolmie also notes that other participants are painting their faces, presumably with the elaborate designs applied on ceremonial occasions by initiate participants and audience members. Many human face masks are decorated with designs which represent actual facial paintings.

Tolmie states that an immense chest is filled with masks and that, with the exception of the bird mask, all of them represent the "human face divine," and an examination of mid-nineteenth-century Heiltsuk masks reveals that by far the majority do represent the human face. The bird dancer is announced by the sound of horns (wooden trumpets), which is mandatory in Northwest Coast performances, and he is costumed in a blanket, kilt and leggings (note Figure 78). The eyes of the bird mask are articulated so that they are lidded with a metal cover. Tolmie records that common masks are called "Nawilock," a Heiltsuk term; in the related Kwak̓wala language, it means "supernatural treasure." This term is absolutely consistent with the concept vested in the Returned-from-Heaven dance cycle of the Heiltsuk and its counterparts, the Tła'sala among the Kwakw<u>aka</u>'wakw and to some degree the Naxnóx̱[10] of the Tsimshian Peoples. In these dances, a reincarnation of an ancestor or spirit power is made manifest through the mask and by the blowing of wooden horns or whistles which represent the ancestral voice and signal the dancer's entrance.

In the 1840s, the Hudson's Bay Company continued to be an important source of ethnographic specimens for other agencies. Company employees provided an array of artifacts, including several masks, to the United States Exploring Expedition when it reached the mouth of the Columbia River in 1841. The collection was ultimately placed in the National Museum of Natural History, Smithsonian Institution. Masks representing a young woman (Figure 33) and an elderly woman (Figure 34) were part of that acquisition, and they bear a strong resemblance, stylistically, to labret-woman masks made by the Kaigani Haida.[11] Written in black ink across the right forehead of both masks is an inscription which reads: "The women of a tribe near Fort Simpson on the NW Coast of America; lat. 54°30″."[12]

34
Haida, Artist Unknown
Mask Representing Woman with Labret, before 1840
24.1 × 19.1 × 11.4
wood and paint
National Museum of Natural History,
Smithsonian Institution, Washington, 2665
Photo by Trevor Mills, Vancouver Art Gallery

33
Haida, Artist Unknown
Mask Representing Young Woman,
before 1840
22.9 × 18.4 × 11.4
wood, metal and paint
National Museum of Natural History,
Smithsonian Institution, Washington, 2667
Photo by Trevor Mills, Vancouver Art Gallery

Truly scientific collecting did not begin until the late nineteenth century. The efforts of James Swan, Johan Adrian Jacobsen, Franz Boas, George Hunt, Charles F. Newcombe, Louis Shotridge, Henry Tate and Marius Barbeau are notable in this period. As ethnographers, they were careful to try to document the context and meaning of works they acquired, allowing us to appreciate with both eye and mind some of the treasures here.

Competing with the professionals at this time was a group of collectors that included government functionaries, senior museum personnel and patrons largely intent on enhancing their personal reputations, missionaries who ostensibly accepted donations which were usually but not always sold to support their ministries, and enthusiasts such as George Gustav Heye who went on to found his own Museum of the American Indian in New York City. By and large, the artifacts they collected are minimally documented and present a challenge to contemporary scholars and First Nations specialists who are working to give such collections the dignity they deserve.

One of the most problematic of these collections is the one acquired for the (now) Canadian Museum of Civilization by Indian Superintendent Israel Powell in 1879. It contains many masks, the majority of which have been designated as Haida. However, an examination of these, on a stylistic basis, places most of them within other traditions. While the Haida acquired certain privileges and the attendant artifacts from their mainland neighbours in the nineteenth century, it is difficult to believe that so many stylistically diverse pieces could have come from Haida Gwaii,[13] the more so as Powell's trip included many stops between northern Vancouver Island and the Nass River.

THE HUMAN FACE DIVINE

By far the majority of masks collected on the Northwest Coast until about 1850 represent a human face or an animal in anthropomorphic guise (Figures 15, 27, 31, 38, 41, 42 and 45). To date, most of those depicting the human face have been categorized as portrait masks, a term that implies the likeness of the visage of a real person is intended. Most of these masks are probably stylized representations of mythic ancestors. In a few examples, however, it is tempting to assume that actual portraiture is intended. The sense of skin and underlying musculature evoked by the mask of a Haida woman wearing a labret (Figure 35) suggests this as a possibility. A Tlingit shaman's mask representing his female spirit helper is similarly naturalistic and may depict a real person.[14]

Nisga'a, Gitxsan and Tsimshian masks used in the Naxnóx dance series are dramatizations of spirit beings. Many of the masks represent human frailties such as conceit (Figure 20), pride, stupidity, avarice, sloth and arrogance. Some categorize social groups such as old people, members of rival tribes, intruders or white men. Others depict

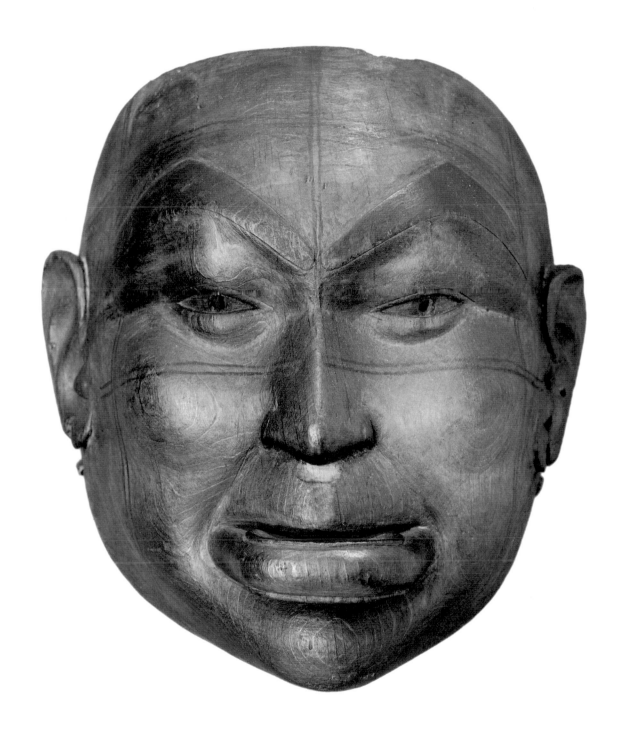

35
Haida, Artist Unknown
Woman Wearing a Labret,
c. 1830
21.0 × 19.7
wood, abalone shell and paint
Photo courtesy Rhode Island School of
Design, Providence, 45.089

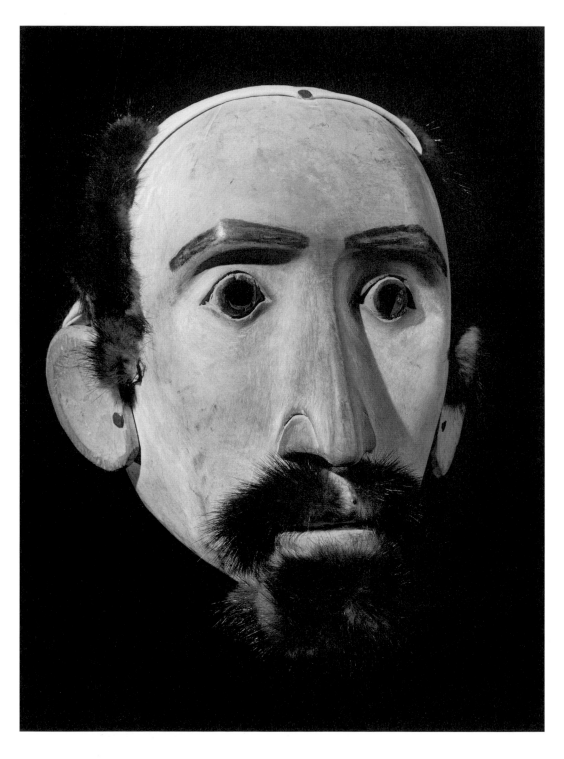

36
Nisg̲a'a, Artist Unknown
Mask Representing White Man,
c. 1880
24.2 × 21.5 × 14.1
wood, cloth, fur, nails and paint
Royal British Columbia Museum, Victoria, 1517
Photo courtesy Royal British Columbia Museum

37 (facing page)
A Haida noblewoman known to
outsiders as "Queen Johnnie" is
wearing a labret and a nose-ring,
both of which indicate her high
rank and status, c. 1884.
Photo by Richard Maynard, courtesy Royal
British Columbia Museum, Victoria, PN5320

an array of animals and celestial objects. Occasionally, they may portray real individuals, as in the case of a Naxnóx mask that appears to be a generic white man with a narrow elongated face, pointed nose, determined lips, small beady eyes and a bald pate (Figure 36). Some Nisga'a people recognize this image as a familiar churchman renowned for his love of rum. As part of an elaborate tableau, an actor wearing this mask appears dressed in a suit, reading from his Bible. As his sermonizing progresses, he removes a bottle from his breast pocket and rapidly becomes intoxicated, eventually falling to the floor in a stupor.

A counterpart Naxnóx mask represents a conceited white woman (Figure 20); during the impersonation, the performer wears a dress with an exaggerated bustle. Obviously, a specific individual was intended by the artist, yet it also reflects a generic human frailty because there are other extant masks representing a "conceited woman." Whether we read conceit or reserved dignity in her face, the visage is a compelling masterpiece of Nisga'a sculpture.

Many of the early human face masks portray noblewomen, so indicated by the large labret placed in the lower lip (Figure 38). This practice was universally remarked upon by early explorers and traders and is frequently illustrated in their journals. Although most outsiders considered the labret tradition repugnant, their fascination was such that many early visitors to the Northwest Coast secured specimens of labrets to display as conversation pieces upon their return home. One such visitor was Captain James Magee, who sailed from Boston aboard the *Margaret* in 1791 to engage in the sea otter trade. On his return, he presented a modest collection of specimens from the Northwest Coast to the Massachusetts Historical Society, including "two Ornaments for the Lips" (Figure 40).[15]

Some contemporary writers have confused the use and distribution of the labret, indicating that it is the prerogative of only noblewomen and that the lip was pierced at birth. The most authoritative summary is supplied by ethnographer George T. Emmons, who indicates that among the Tlingit, the perforation was made when a girl reached puberty.[16] At that time, a small hole was made in her lower lip and a nail-shaped bone plug was inserted. After about 1830, this "training labret" (Figure 39) was often made of silver, the precious material having been acquired through trade. Emmons emphasized that among the Tlingit, all women with the exception of slaves wore labrets. Although medium-sized labrets "were universally worn by women of middle age and low rank,"[17] the largest (of a size represented in Figures 41 and 42) were worn only by elderly women of high rank (Figure 37).

38 (facing page)
Haida, Artist Unknown
Mask Representing Djilakons, an
Eagle Moiety Ancestor,
before 1826
26.0 × 20.0 × 14.0
wood and paint
Peabody Museum of Archeology and
Ethnology, Harvard University, Cambridge,
10/76826
Photo by Hillel Burger, courtesy Peabody
Museum, Harvard University

39 (top)
Haida, Simeon Stilthda*
Mask Representing Young Woman,
c. 1870
22.5 × 18.0 × 10.2
wood, string, metal and paint
Royal British Columbia Museum, Victoria,
10666
Photo by Trevor Mills, Vancouver Art Gallery

40 (bottom)
Haida, Artist Unknown
Labret, before 1794
2.0 × 8.0 × 5.0
wood
Peabody Museum of Archeology and
Ethnology, Harvard University, Cambridge,
10/277
Photo by Hillel Burger, courtesy Peabody
Museum, Harvard University

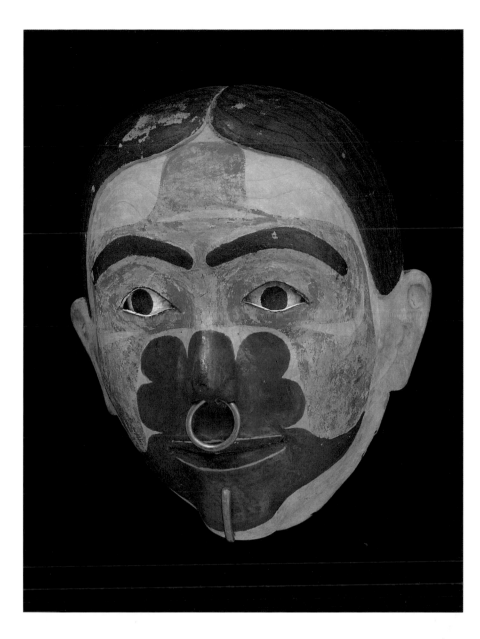

Of the many masks representing women with labrets, none has been celebrated in recent scholarship more than a suite of masks and associated figures (Figures 15, 38, 41, 43 and 44) created by a particular artist from a northern group. According to scholar Bill Holm, "A number of these masks were certainly the work of a single carver, whose sculptural and painting style is recognized by a combination of unique features: round, open eyes with a grooved upper lid; large eye socket; small, narrow nose flattened under the nostrils; rounded, sometimes double chin; wide mouth with very large labret. The face painting is expertly designed in blue and red. Some of the masks in this group have large, elaborately carved ears, painted red."[18]

The prototype of these masks is hereafter referred to as the "Jenna Cass" type (Figure 38). This prototype is significant because all evidence points to the fact it was produced for sale, presaging a commercial market and a type of mask which continued to be made well into the twentieth century. Inside the mask is an inscription that reads "A correct likeness of Jenna Cass, a high chief woman of the Northwest Coast" and a signature interpreted as "J. Goodwin, Esq." Holm has suggested the seemingly Euroamerican name Jenna Cass was probably the collector's attempt to render the Haida word Djilakons, the name of an ancestress of the Eagle moiety of the Haida.[19] Her exploits were noted by ethnologist John R. Swanton, who writes, "Djiláqons is a conspicuous and ever recurring figure in their mythology" and "All the Eagles upon this island came in succession out of womb of Djiláqons. In the process of descent they became differentiated [into the various families]."[20]

A sister mask (Figure 15), donated by Captain Daniel Cross a year later in 1827 to the East India Marine Society in Salem, Massachusetts, has an equally tantalizing description in a printed catalogue dated 1831: "Wooden mask once used by a distinguished chieftainess of the Indians at Nootka Sound—said to represent exactly the manner in which she painted her face."[21]

New information about these two masks has recently come to light. The prototype Jenna Cass mask (Figure 38) probably was presented by one I. (Isaac) Goodwin rather than J. Goodwin to the American Antiquarian Society (and later transferred to the Peabody Museum at Harvard University). Isaac Goodwin is thought to have personally made the entry in its first ledger catalogue.[22] Dated November 1, 1826, it reads: "A carved representation of the face of a high chief female, on the Northwest Coast. Carved and painted by a native of that coast. Presented to the Society by I. Goodwin, Esq. of Worcester." Goodwin, who was a lawyer and a postmaster by profession and an avid antiquarian by avocation, probably had never visited the Northwest Coast and may have been given the mask by an associate or forebear. His catalogue entry, combined with his inscription inside the mask, clearly indicates a familiarity with the actual carving.

A search of the archives at the Peabody Essex Museum has proved rewarding. While the published 1831 catalogue of the East India Marine Society of Salem indicates the sister mask (Figure 15) had a Nootka Sound provenance, an earlier handwritten entry in the archives, dated March 7—May 3, 1827, reads: "1 Indian mask, representing the features of an aged female of the Casern tribe on the N.W. Coast of America. Captain Daniel Cross of Beverly." The "Casern tribe" can only be a Kaigani Haida group who occupied Kasaan village in Alaska. A speaker of English usually hears the long "a" sound in Northwest Coast languages as "aar." Supporting evidence comes from the log of the brig *Griffon*, which several times put into "Casern" and Kaigani. On August 22, 1825, she bears for Kaigani where her crew is "employed shipping furs on board the *Rob Roy* for China."[23] The donor of the Jenna Cass prototype mask, Daniel Cross, was in command of the *Rob Roy* upon his return to Boston in 1827.[24] With reasonable certainty, we can now link this mask with the Kaigani Haida village of Kasaan and suggest the maker was resident there.

If we accept that the two Jenna Cass masks are from the hand of a single Kaigani master carver, we need to expand on Holm's physical description. Notable on all of the masks is a solid design element in red, which begins at the bridge of the nose on the right-hand side of the face and tapers to a fine point on the lower cheek. Consistent as well are the solid broad line of paint which commences at the right temple and flows down the jaw line to terminate in the middle of the chin, the structure of the painted design across the forehead, and the preference for continuous scalloping. The distinctly modeled, rounded projecting chin is another notable feature.

Another group of three labret-woman masks (Figures 33, 34 and 42) might be mistaken as companions of the two Jenna Cass type examples, but careful examination detects enough differences to conclude these are the work of an associated but separate artist or group of artists. Disparate details include a more elongate and oval face, ears which are consistent in this suite yet quite different from those on some of the prototypes, an angled rather than an arched upper lip, significantly smaller labrets, and less precisely conceived and applied painted designs. In the main, these are less well documented than the Jenna Cass type, and they begin to appear on the scene about a decade later in the late 1830s. Like the Jenna Cass examples, most of them are not rigged for use and show no signs of having been worn.

The popularity of the labret-woman image is reinforced by a stylistically distinct example (Figure 45). This is obviously a separate substyle, but because it was apparently collected in 1831, it must be considered a contemporary of the Jenna Cass type.

In the 1870s, we can begin to name some of the Haida artists who were creating masks for sale. Slightly smaller than masks made by their forebears and depicting men as well as women (Figures 39, 46, 47, 48 and 49), the majority appear to have been made by the Haida artist Simeon Stilthda, who died in 1883. At one time they were thought to have been made a contemporary of his, Charles Gwaytihl,[25] but Holm discovered evidence suggesting that Stilthda, rather than Gwaytihl, was the author of this suite.

41
Haida, Artist Unknown
Mask Representing Djilakons,
c. 1830
19.5 × 15.0 × 5.5
wood and paint
Peabody Museum of Archeology and
Ethnology, Harvard University, Cambridge,
10/51671
Photo by Hillel Burger, courtesy Peabody
Museum, Harvard University

42
Haida, Artist Unknown
*Mask Representing Noble Woman
Wearing Labret,* c. 1840
20.9 × 22.9 × 11.1
wood, paint and glass beads
University of Pennsylvania Museum of
Archaeology and Anthropology, Philadelphia,
45-15-2
Photo courtesy University of Pennsylvania
Museum

43
Haida, Artist Unknown
Mask Representing Djilakons,
c. 1830
17.1 × 16.5 × 13.9
wood and paint
National Museum of Natural History,
Smithsonian Institution, Washington, 2666
Photo by Trevor Mills, Vancouver Art Gallery

44
Haida, Artist Unknown
Figure Representing Djilakons,
c. 1830
20.0 × 8.5 × 5.5
wood, hair and paint
Peabody Museum of Archeology and
Ethnology, Harvard University, Cambridge,
10/53093
Photo by Hillel Burger, courtesy Peabody
Museum, Harvard University

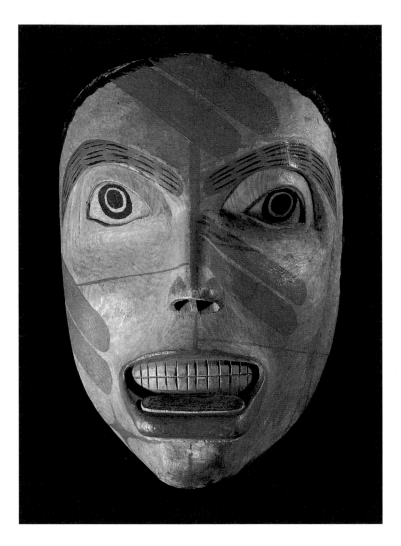

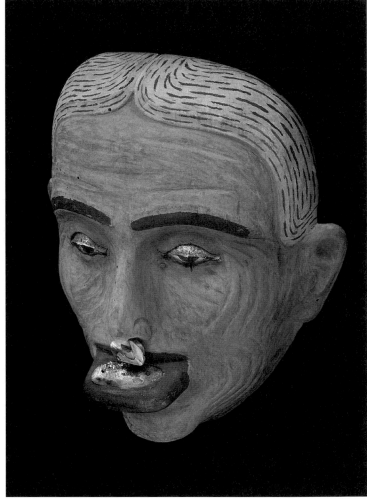

45
Haida, Artist Unknown
*Mask Representing Noble Woman
with Labret*, before 1831
21.5 × 16.5 × 11.0
wood and paint
McCord Museum of Canadian History,
Montréal, M 10390
Photo courtesy Musée McCord Museum

46
Haida, Simeon Stilthda*
*Mask Representing Elderly Noble
Woman*, c. 1870
23.0 × 20.2 × 11.0
wood, abalone shell, leather and string
Royal British Columbia Museum, Victoria,
10671
Photo by Trevor Mills, Vancouver Art Gallery

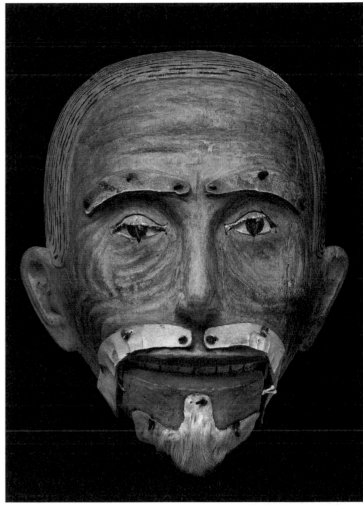

47
Haida, Simeon Stilthda*
*Mask Representing Elderly
Woman*, c. 1870
23.6 × 18.4 × 11.4
wood, abalone shell, leather, string and paint
McMichael Canadian Art Collection,
Kleinburg, 1981.103
Photo by Trevor Mills, Vancouver Art Gallery

48
Haida, Simeon Stilthda*
Mask Representing Elderly Man,
c. 1870
23.2 × 20.0 × 11.0
wood, hide, fur, nails, string and paint
Royal British Columbia Museum, Victoria,
10670
Photo by Trevor Mills, Vancouver Art Gallery

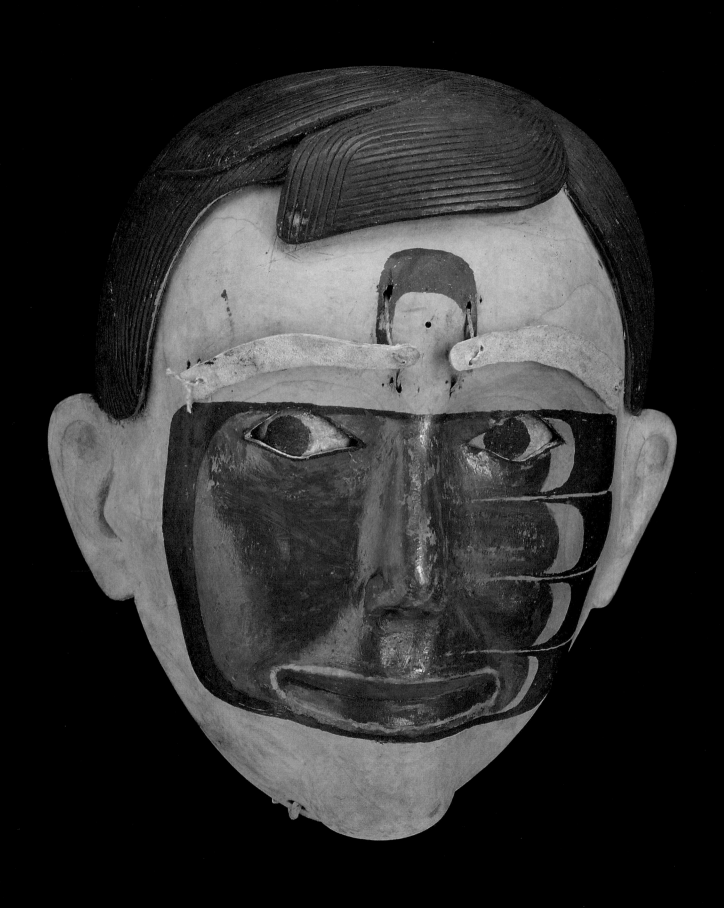

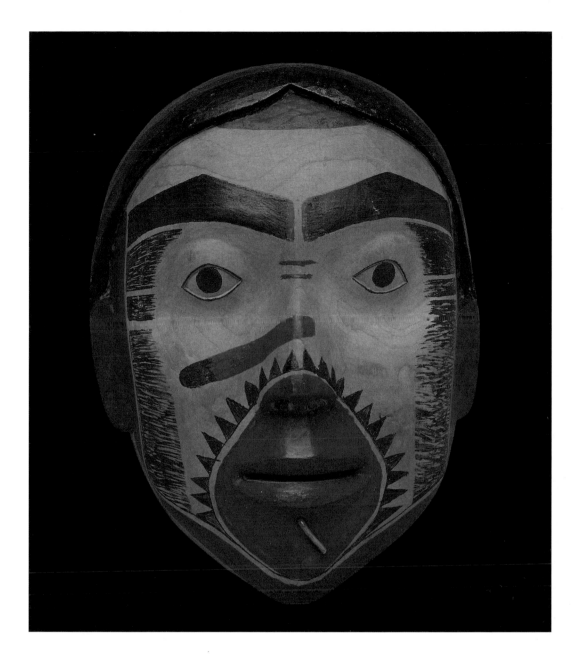

49 (facing page)
Haida, Simeon Stilthda*
Mask Representing Young Man,
c. 1870
24.1 × 20.6 × 11.6
wood, hide, nails and paint
Royal British Columbia Museum, Victoria,
10665
Photo by Trevor Mills, Vancouver Art Gallery

50
Haida, John Gwaytihl
Mask Representing Young Woman
Wearing Training Labret, 1882
29.2 × 46.2 × 61.7
wood, metal and paint
American Museum of Natural History, New
York, 16/364
Photo by Trevor Mills, Vancouver Art Gallery

Recent research by Robin Wright reveals that Gwaytihl's first name was John rather than Charles, as has previously been recorded.[26]

About two dozen masks by Stilthda are known, and they are more naturalistically rendered than any other Northwest Coast examples. Size and proportion are lifelike, with only the eyebrows stylized in typical Northwest Coast fashion. All have rounded, wonderfully modeled chins, which appear to be vestiges of the Jenna Cass type; all but those representing the elderly have facial paintings; and all have either eyes, eyelids, eyebrows or mouths that move. The inside rigging to operate these movable components is so complex and takes up so much space that it is impossible to consider these masks ever could have been worn.

John Gwaytihl did carve the labret-woman mask represented in Figure 50. Inside, it is inscribed: "carved by Quaa-telth, Masset, Qⁿ Char. Is., 1882." Although subtle, the

51
Makah*, Artist Unknown
Mask Representing Woman,
c. 1880
27.9 × 30.5 × 11.4
wood, hair, yarn and string
National Museum of Natural History,
Smithsonian Institution, Washington, 4118
Photo by Trevor Mills, Vancouver Art Gallery

52
Haida, John Cross
*Mask Representing Eagle Down
Woman*, c. 1900
30.3 × 29.8 × 14.8
wood, nails and paint
Vancouver Museum, Vancouver, AA93
Photo by Trevor Mills, Vancouver Art Gallery

differences in form and proportion are evident enough to distinguish it from the Stilthda examples. The most notable distinction is in the facial painting, which is conceived and applied in a manner radically different from that on the others.

A female portrait mask collected by James Swan (Figure 51) is stylistically Makah, but structurally and conceptually bears a close resemblance to the masks by Stilthda. Elements favoured by Stilthda include eyes which move horizontally, an articulated lower jaw, strands of red wool placed in holes drilled through the ears (a Haida custom) and facial painting. It is difficult not to conclude that a Makah carver viewed a Stilthda mask owned by Swan (whose office and home had many Northwest Coast collectibles on exhibit) and was inspired, perhaps with Swan's encouragement, to make this version forwarded by Swan to the Smithsonian Institution.

As far as those Haida artists who grew up in a traditional context are concerned, perhaps the final work representing a labret-woman is illustrated in Figure 52. While not as elegant as its predecessors, it demonstrates the tenacity of the tradition. A label inside, dated 11-4-46, reads: "40 years old. Carver John Cross. Skidegate Mission . . . Eagle Down Woman." A horizontal bite piece inside this mask, collected in 1906, exhibits teeth marks, indicating that it was used ceremonially (Figure 32).

While most of the humanoid masks representing women appear to have been made for sale, many others from the same time period were produced for Native use. Like the nontraditional examples, they are mostly made by the northernmost Northwest Coast groups, the Tlingit, Haida and Tsimshian Peoples. The sensitively made Nisg̱a'a Eagle Woman (Figure 54) is typical, as are those in Figures 53, 55 and 56.

Masks collected through the mid-nineteenth century representing males, presumably ancestors, appear in considerable numbers, but few of these seem to have been made for the collectors' market. The seminal eighteenth century Nuu-chah-nulth examples (Figures 27 and 31) are elegant in their restrained simplicity, and the mask shown in Figure 57, while collected about 1895, may be of a similar age. By the 1860s, Nuu-chah-nulth humanoid masks had become triangular in cross-section rather than frontally aligned as in the archaic types. Increasingly, they were decorated with geometric designs, a practice that continued into the twentieth century (Figures 28, 29 and 58).

Heiltsuk masks from the early to mid-nineteenth century representing males include several subtypes, but the facial painting and flat, projecting stylized ears are found consistently throughout (Figures 59 and 61). The stylistic overlap between the Heiltsuk, Haisla and southern Coast Tsimshian often dictates a generic central coast designation.

53
Tsimshian*, Artist
Unknown
*Naxnóx Mask Representing
Woman*, 19th century
22.5 × 20.8 × 11.3
wood, abalone shell and paint
McMichael Canadian Art Collection,
Kleinburg, 1979.5
Photo by Trevor Mills, Vancouver Art Gallery

54 (facing page)
Tsimshian, Artist Unknown
*Mask Representing Young Girl
with Braids*, c. 1860
30.8 × 20.6 × 14.0
wood, hair, cedar bark, twine and paint
Portland Art Museum, Portland, 46.14
Photo by Eduardo Calderon

55 (facing page)
Tsimshian (attrib.), Artist Unknown
Naxnóx Mask Representing Human, 19th century
23.1 × 18.3 × 7.9
wood and paint
McMichael Canadian Art Collection, Kleinburg, 1978.21.2
Photo by Trevor Mills, Vancouver Art Gallery

56
Haida, Artist Unknown
Mask Representing Young Woman, c. 1860
20.8 × 17.3 × 9.2
wood, abalone shell and paint
Canadian Museum of Civilization, Hull, VII B 928 a,b
Photo courtesy Canadian Museum of Civilization, s85-3284

57
Nuu-chah-nulth, Artist
Unknown
Mask Representing Male, early
19th century
16.0 × 14.5 × 8.0
wood and paint
Canadian Museum of Civilization, Hull,
VII-F-230
Photo courtesy Canadian Museum of
Civilization, 75-9427

58
Nuu-chah-nulth, Clayoquot
Artist*
*Mask Representing Male
Ancestor*, c. 1870
30.0 × 19.0
wood, hair and paint
Canadian Museum of Civilization, Hull,
VII C 2
Photo courtesy Canadian Museum of
Civilization, 72-5372

59
Heiltsuk*, Artist Unknown
Mask Representing Ancestral Human, c. 1870
27.0 × 23.5 × 14.5
wood and paint
McCord Museum of Canadian History,
Montréal, ME 982.32.1
Photo courtesy Musée McCord Museum

60 (facing page)
Nuxalk, Artist Unknown
Mask Representing Sun, c. 1870
160.0 diameter
wood and paint
American Museum of Natural History, New
York, 16/1507
Photo by Trevor Mills, Vancouver Art Gallery

63 (facing page)
Tsimshian, Artist Unknown
*Human Face Mask Representing
Male*, c. 1870
23.2 × 19.1 × 12.7
wood and paint
Seattle Art Museum, Gift of John H.
Hauberg, Seattle, 91.1.39
Photo by Paul Macapia, courtesy Seattle Art
Museum

64
Haida, Artist Unknown
Mask Representing Male Ancestor,
before 1840
26.0 × 20.3 × 12.7
wood and paint
National Museum of Natural History,
Smithsonian Institution, Washington,
73332B
Photo by Trevor Mills, Vancouver Art Gallery

65
Tlingit*, Artist Unknown
Figure Representing Man, c. 1870
17.8 × 8.9 × 9.2
wood and paint
National Museum of Natural History,
Smithsonian Institution, Washington,
13102
Photo by Trevor Mills, Vancouver Art Gallery

66 (facing page)
Haida, Artist Unknown
Mask Representing Male Ancestor,
c. 1850, collected in 1879
26.5 × 21.5
wood, hide, bone, nails and paint
Canadian Museum of Civilization, Hull,
VII-B-3
Photo courtesy Canadian Museum of
Civilization, s85-3270

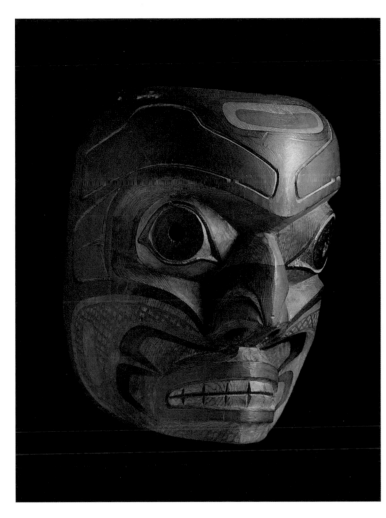

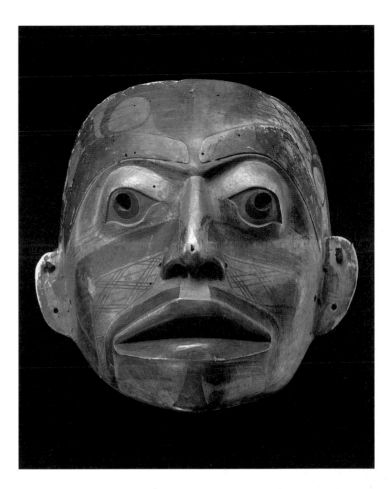

69
Heiltsuk, Artist Unknown
Mask Representing Male Ancestor,
c. 1865
28.0 × 28.8 × 15.0
wood and paint
Canadian Museum of Civilization, Hull,
VII-D-25
Photo courtesy Canadian Museum of
Civilization, s98-363

67 (facing page)
Kwakw<u>aka</u>'wakw, Willie
Seaweed
Mask Representing a Speaker,
c. 1930
28.5 × 19.0 × 14.0
yellow cedar and paint
Campbell River Museum, Campbell River,
992.13
Photo by Trevor Mills, Vancouver Art Gallery

68
Kwakw<u>aka</u>'wakw, Tony Hunt
Mask Representing Male Ancestor,
1967
26.1 × 20.4 × 15.6
red cedar and paint
Royal British Columbia Museum, Victoria,
18913
Photo by Trevor Mills, Vancouver Art Gallery

70
Tsimshian, Artist Unknown
Mask Representing Male, c. 1870
21.0 × 16.5 × 9.5
wood and paint
Canadian Museum of Civilization, Hull,
VII-C-314
Photo courtesy Canadian Museum of
Civilization, s98-364

71 (facing page)
Tsimshian, Artist Unknown
*Mask Representing Naxnóx
Spirit*, c. 1870
23.0 × 28.0 × 23.0
wood, copper, hair and paint
Canadian Museum of Civilization, Hull,
VII-C-1804
Photo courtesy Canadian Museum of
Civilization, s98-365

THE COSMOS

In the Northwest Coast cosmos, there are four realms, identified somewhat arbitrarily as the Sky World, the Undersea World, the Mortal World and the Spirit World. Each tribe does not necessarily consider its universe to consist absolutely of these four; among some, the concepts may be more fluid or less inclusive. The inhabitants of these worlds are spirit powers that can move from one domain to another or have counterparts in another.

THE SKY WORLD

While all four domains in the Northwest Coast cosmos are significant, in many ways the Sky World dominates legend and life (Figure 73 to 103). Ancestral heroes descended from the heavens, landing with a blinding aura when they transformed into humans. The Heiltsuk, originators of many of the dances found among their neighbours to the north, south and east, have a dance series called Dhuẃláẋa, which they translate as "Returned-from-Heaven." In it, ancestral beings depart this world and are transported to the heavens, from whence they return to materialize in recognizable form. Most of the surviving masks in this series depict humans, supporting Tolmie's observation that many of them represent "the human face divine." Others are recognizable as undersea, mortal or spirit creatures such as *pk̓vs*, the "wild man of the woods" (Figure 72).

 The Returned-from-Heaven/transformation concept is articulated in a pair of spectacular masks with a common inspiration. Stylistically, one appears to be Heiltsuk, especially given the liberal application of parallel dashing, much of it in red (Figure 22A), a central coast device that is found more in Heiltsuk and Tsimshian examples than any other tribal style. The other is reliably attributed as Nuxalk (Figure 74A), and the central human face fits clearly within the Nuxalk sculptural tradition. Attribution notwithstanding, the transformation from bird to inner human, whose serene yet commanding face can stand alone or expand to incorporate the surrounding corona (creating a personified celestial orb), is one of the great accomplishments of Northwest Coast art.

 The Tsimshian Peoples and the Haida visualize the sky as a great dome arching over a flat, circular earth. The sun, moon and stars are suspended from the top edge of this firmament and move in limited paths about it. Great houses are situated in the sky, occupied by diverse powers. The Haida recognize an ultimate celestial force which John R. Swanton translates as the "Power of the Shining Heavens."[27] This authority is considered an all-seeing protector from whom those in need may seek supplication. While each tribal group appears to have an omnipotent deity, there is no clearly defined celestial hierarchy below that power. It is difficult to find an English-language equivalent to describe these powers, but the word deity, in the sense of "heavenly creature," will suffice.

72
Heiltsuk, Artist Unknown
Mask Representing Pk̓vs, c. 1880
50.1 × 32.0 × 20.7
wood, horsehair, leather, nails and paint
McMichael Canadian Art Collection,
Kleinburg, 1984.5
Photo by Trevor Mills, Vancouver Art Gallery

The Nuxalk appear to have developed this concept more elaborately than any other coastal group. Near the upper edge of their Sky World, a supreme deity occupies a great house called Nusmata ("the place of origin of myths and legends"). This ultimate power is the Sun (Figures 23 and 60); at a certain point in distant time, he sent four supernatural carpenters to this world to create human life and an environment to provide for them. These masks that appear to represent the ancestral sun could be worn by dancers, but they also might have been used as theatrical props and rigged to move across the rear wall of the ceremonial house to indicate the daily passage of this celestial power.

The distant heights of the Sky World may be reached in several ways by land-bound myth people. The usual way is by means of a flight of arrows. The first arrow penetrates the edge of an entryway to the uppermost region, and successive ones are shot to form a chain, linked point to notch, enabling the adventurer to climb up. Others can fly though the hole in the sky if they are quick and agile enough, and if they perform a brief ritual beforehand.[28] Some traditions identify the arc of the rainbow as a means to access and leave the heavens. Others say the Milky Way is an infinite spiral down which the soul travels from birth to oblivion. The Kwakwaka'wakw call this concentration of distant stars "the seam of heaven," and they identify other constellations, notably Orion and the Pleiades, as representing sea otter hunters and their canoes, lost and frozen in the night sky.[29]

To the Haida, the celestial bodies—sun, moon and stars—are inanimate objects[30] and, with the exception of the Moon as a crest image, are rarely represented in their art. Among the Nisga'a, Gitxsan and Tsimshian on the adjacent mainland, the Moon is found extensively as a mask (Figures 1, 21 and 103) as well as a crest image.

The Kwakwaka'wakw view the Sun as an old man who walks in slow, stately grace across the sky every day (Figures 25, 26, 82 and 101). He may wear abalone pendants in his ears and a blanket festooned with that lustrous shell. During mythic times, a ray of sun penetrated a woman, thus impregnating her, and she soon gave birth to Mink, the mischievous son of the Sun. Mink eventually reached the heavens, where his father assigned him the responsibility of walking the daily route wearing the abalone blanket. Predictably, for those familiar with his many antics, Mink darted quickly across the sky, causing his aunts, the clouds, to part so that the waters below boiled and forests flamed.

Three Sun masks attributed to Kwakwaka'wakw artist Charlie James (c. 1870–1938) demonstrate that the making of masks for sale continued into the twentieth century. One is a transforming Sun (Figure 26), made about 1906 for a 'Namgis (Nimpkish) chief. A second (Figure 82) is part of the "Potlatch Collection"[31] of masks surrendered under duress to Indian Agent William Halliday in 1922. The third well-documented work (Figure 73) was made about 1930 for sale directly to a curio dealer. A handsome, competent carving, it nonetheless incorporates many of the shortcuts employed by James in his commercial products,[32] as well as the finishing coat of shellac.

73
Kwakw<u>a</u>ka'wakw, Charlie James
Mask Representing Sun, c. 1930
47.0 × 51.4 × 17.8
yellow cedar and paint
Burke Museum of Natural History and
Culture, University of Washington, Seattle,
Walter Waters Collection, 25.0/440
Photo courtesy Burke Museum of Natural
History and Culture

74A
Nuxalk, Artist Unknown
(closed view)
Sun Transformation Mask,
c. 1865
wood, hair, twine and paint
Linden-Museum Stuttgart—Staatliches
Museum für Völkerkunde, Stuttgart,
19178
Photo by Anatol Dreyer, courtesy Linden-
Museum Stuttgart

74B (facing page)
Nuxalk, Artist Unknown
(open view)
Sun Transformation Mask,
c. 1865
78.0 × 100.0
wood, hair, twine and paint
Linden-Museum Stuttgart—Staatliches
Museum für Völkerkunde, Stuttgart, 19178
Photo by Anatol Dreyer, courtesy Linden-
Museum Stuttgart

Below the outer extreme are skies inhabited by fabulous birds, of which the most universal is the Thunderbird. In a generalized way, all Northwest Coast groups say that when these mythic avians ruffle their feathers, they cause the rumble of thunder, and when they blink their eyes, lightning flashes earthward. This interpretation is recorded as early as 1834 by W. F. Tolmie, who asked Chief Boston "what thunder and lightning were occasioned by—he answered—By a large bird which on awakening suddenly flaps its wings, thus causing thunder & flashes lightning from its eyes."[33] Some Kwakwaka'wakw prefer to think of these supernatural birds as a race of sky-dwelling people who roll great boulders around the heavens; when the rocks collide, thunder is produced.

Thunderbirds have particular identities and are associated with specific village groups or with individual lineages. No single family would dare to claim a Thunderbird image other than their very own, which has a site-specific place of origin, a unique name and details of form and visage that are not necessarily shared. Thus, the Hesquiaht, a Nuu-chah-nulth tribe, have a named Thunderbird which appeared as a brilliant flash in a blinding hailstorm, barely visible as it landed at low tide on a rock off the village foreshore. When the weather cleared, its great talon marks, scratched on the stony surface, confirmed its passing; they can still be seen today as a reminder of that ancestor.

In a late nineteenth-century Nuu-chah-nulth Thunderbird forehead mask, the creature is characterized by the feathered plumes which extend above the head. Artist Art Thompson of the Dididaht tribe of the Nuu-chah-nulth chose to represent the Thunderbird in its human persona (Figures 76 and 77); stylized feathers and sheets of rain are represented in the facial painting, and the eyes revolve rapidly to reveal a copper orb, suggesting the flash of lightning.

The Thunderbird claimed by the 'Namgis people in Kwakwaka'wakw territory flew out of the heavens to assist a man who had transformed from a giant halibut.[34] Upon finishing its task, the bird also transformed to human, then removed its Thunderbird headdress and winged cape, sending them back to the upper sky. This mask may be worn projecting from the forehead, revealing the dancer's face to indicate the duality of bird and man, or it can cover the performer's face and be completed with a full costume (Figure 78). Robert Joseph's essay in this book recounts another Kwakwaka'wakw version of a Thunderbird genesis.

The Thunderbird has younger brothers, notably the Kulus (Figures 75 and 100), which first appeared in our world atop a mountain, covered with dazzling down.

Other supernatural birds inhabit the middle heavens, attendants of the Kwakwaka'wakw cannibal spirit Baxwbakwalanuxwsiwe' (Cannibal-at-the-North-End-of-the-World). These birds originated in the Heiltsuk shaman's dance series (ćaíqa) which, like the Returned-from-Heaven cycle, spread through intermarriage and acquisition through warfare to surrounding neighbours. The primary servants to the cannibal spirit are the

Huxwhukw (Figures 13, 79, 80 and 95), the supernatural Raven (Figure 83) and the Crooked-Beak (Figures 14, 81, 85 to 88 and 92). One archaic Heiltsuk example of the Crooked-Beak (Figure 84) is elegant, minimal and understated. Probably dating from 1865, it is a forerunner of the more elaborate and flamboyant early to mid-twentieth-century Kwakwaka'wakw versions.

75
Kwakwaka'wakw, Tom Hunt
*Forehead Mask Representing
Kulus*, 1985
30.5 × 44.5 × 23.0
red cedar, yellow cedar, cedar bark and paint
Private Collection
Photo by Trevor Mills, Vancouver Art Gallery

76 (facing page)
Nuu-chah-nulth, Art Thompson
*Mask Representing Thunderbird in
Human Form*, 1986
33.0 × 23.0 × 21.0
red cedar, copper, rope, red cedar bark and paint
Royal British Columbia Museum, Victoria,
18293
Photo by Trevor Mills, Vancouver Art Gallery

77
Nuu-chah-nulth, Art Thompson
*Mask Representing Thunderbird in
Human Form*, 1989
63.0 × 26.0 × 26.0
red cedar, cedar bark, eagle feathers, horsehair,
copper, leather, nylon twine, plywood, screws
and paint
Spirit Wrestler Gallery, Vancouver
Photo by Trevor Mills, Vancouver Art Gallery

78
Kwakwaka'wakw, Calvin Hunt
Thunderbird Costume, 1982
200.6 × 124.4 × 78.7
cedar, cedar bark, canvas, feathers, nails and
paint
University of British Columbia, Museum of
Anthropology, Vancouver, 863/1-4
Photo by Greg Osadchuk, courtesy *The
Province*, Pacific Press Limited, Vancouver

79 (facing page)
**Kwakw<u>a</u>ka'wakw,
Bill Henderson**
Mask Representing Huxwhukw,
1991
38.0 × 33.0 × 168.0
red cedar, alder, cedar bark, leather, nails,
screws, staples, nylon twine and paint
Private Collection
Photo by Trevor Mills, Vancouver Art Gallery

80
Kwakw<u>a</u>ka'wakw, Henry Speck
Mask Representing Huxwhukw,
c. 1985
22.0 × 26.0 × 151.0
red cedar, cedar bark, leather, nails, wire,
nylon twine and paint
Private Collection
Photo by Trevor Mills, Vancouver Art Gallery

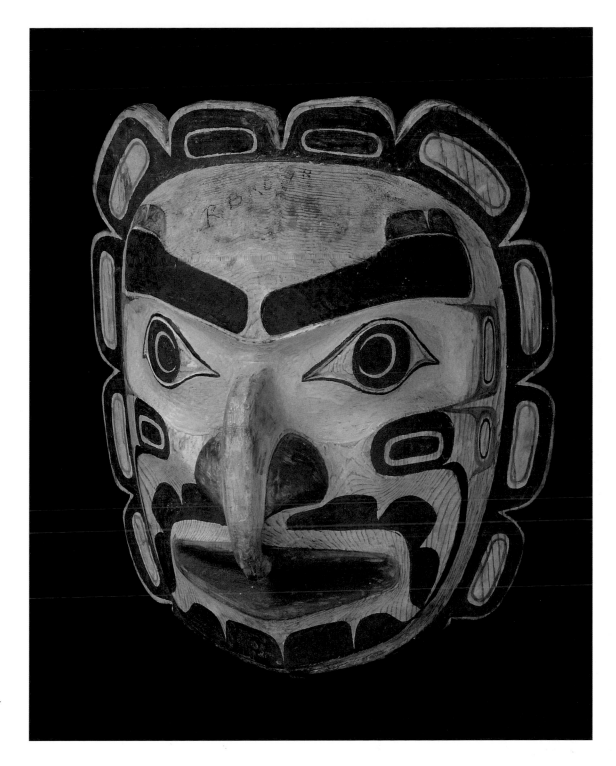

81 (facing page)
Kwakw<u>aka</u>'wakw, Tony Hunt
Mask Representing Crooked-Beak,
1980
77.0 × 25.0 × 94.0
red cedar, cedar bark, raffia, leather, nails,
nylon twine and paint
Private Collection
Photo by Trevor Mills, Vancouver Art Gallery

82
Kwakw<u>aka</u>'wakw,
Charlie James*
Mask Representing Sun, c. 1915
40.5 × 35.2 × 24.5
red cedar, cotton twine, rubber and paint
U'mista Cultural Centre, Alert Bay, 80.01.131
Photo by Trevor Mills, Vancouver Art Gallery

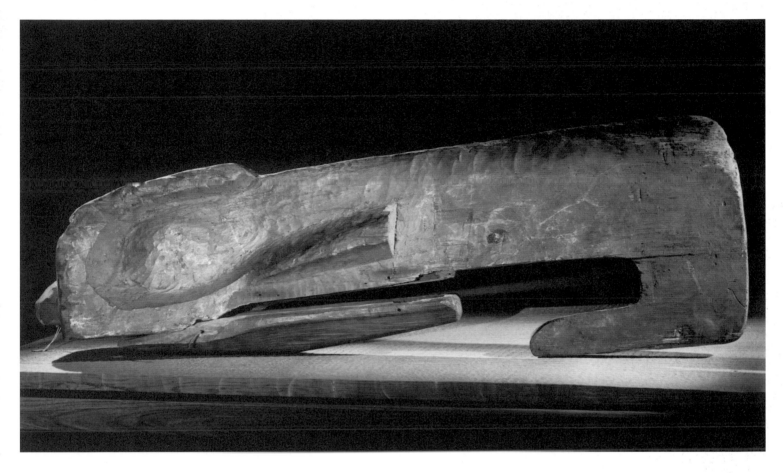

83 (facing page)
Kwakw<u>a</u>ka'wakw, Henry Speck
*Mask Representing Cannibal
Raven*, 1993
35.0 × 25.5 × 123.0
red cedar, cedar bark, leather, nails, nylon
twine and paint
Collection of Dr. Granger Avery and Mrs.
Winnie Avery
Photo by Trevor Mills, Vancouver Art Gallery

84
Heiltsuk, Artist Unknown
*Mask Representing Cannibal
Bird*, c. 1865
48.0 × 29.2 × 149.0
red cedar, iron and paint
Royal British Columbia Museum, Victoria, 8
Photo courtesy Royal British Columbia
Museum

85
Kwak<u>wa</u>ka'wakw,
Bill Henderson
Mask Representing Crooked-Beak,
1992
65.0 × 28.0 × 76.0
red cedar, cedar bark, leather, nails, twine
and paint
Private Collection
Photo by Trevor Mills, Vancouver Art Gallery

86 (facing page)
Kwak<u>wa</u>ka'wakw, Henry Speck
Mask Representing Crooked-Beak,
1983
55.0 × 28.0 × 101.0
red cedar, cedar bark, nylon twine, leather
and paint
Collection of Dr. Granger Avery and Mrs.
Winnie Avery
Photo by Trevor Mills, Vancouver Art Gallery

87
Kwakw<u>aka</u>'wakw, Willie Seaweed
Mask Representing Crooked-Beak,
1940
103.0 × 29.0 × 90.0
red cedar, cedar bark, nails, leather, twine and
paint
Royal British Columbia Museum, Victoria,
17377
Photo courtesy Royal British Columbia
Museum

88 (facing page)
Kwakw<u>aka</u>'wakw, George Hunt Jr.
Mask Representing Crooked-Beak,
1989
88.0 × 93.0 × 24.0
red cedar, cedar bark, horsehair, copper,
abalone shell, leather, nylon twine and paint
Private Collection
Photo by Trevor Mills, Vancouver Art Gallery

The influence of Kwakw<u>aka</u>'wakw artist Willie Seaweed (c. 1873–1967) on the contemporary generation has been considerable. His Crooked-Beak mask (Figure 87) has inspired literally dozens of modern versions made both for the art market and for traditional use. Modified versions incorporating Seaweed design elements or concepts by Tony Hunt (Figure 81) and Henry Speck (Figure 86) are fine examples of the latter. While incorporating Seaweed elements such as the eye structure and cheek, George Hunt Jr. has redefined Seaweed's flamboyant style in a unique and personal fashion (Figure 88). Henry Speck is perhaps the leading iconoclast among makers of Hamat̓sa masks. He has translated his late father Ozistalis's individualistic two-dimensional style, which evolved in narrative paintings, into a three-dimensional form dictated by the flat designs rather than by the carved planes.

The Kwakw<u>aka</u>'wakw version of the cannibal dance series (T̓sek̲a or Red Cedar Bark dance), and the attendant cannibal bird (Hamat̓sa) masks, has become predominant. The main reason is because the Kwakw<u>aka</u>'wakw were able to withstand the considerable pressure from civil and religious authorities to abandon their traditional ceremonial ways. This is not to suggest that other groups were left bereft of memory and practice— far from it—but the massive assemblage of Kwakw<u>aka</u>'wakw material culture relating to ceremony that has survived since systematic collecting began in the 1880s is a testament to the extent to which their art flourished over the past century.

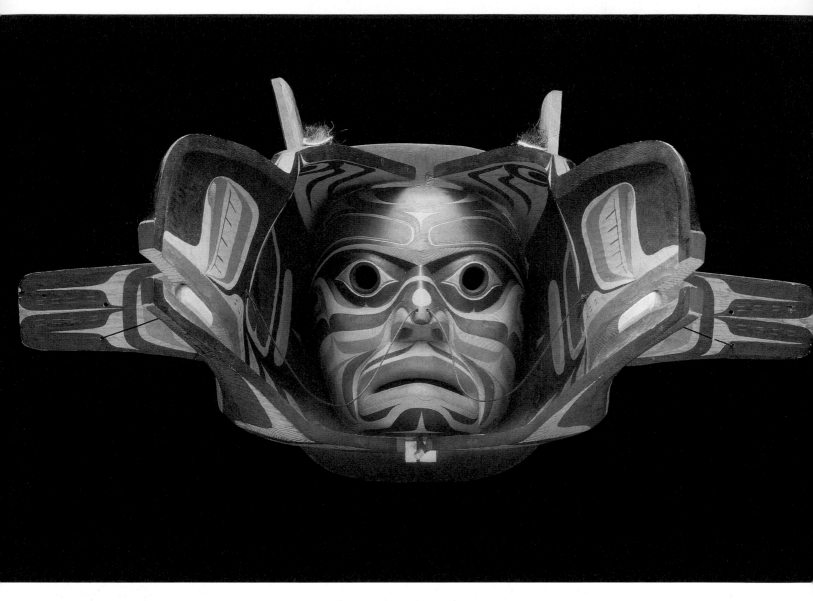

89
Kwakwa̱ka'wakw, Mervyn Child
(open view)
Raven Transformation Mask,
1980
35.0 × 79.0 × 61.0
red cedar, horsehair, cloth, nylon twine,
plastic lens and paint
Private Collection
Photo by Trevor Mills, Vancouver Art Gallery

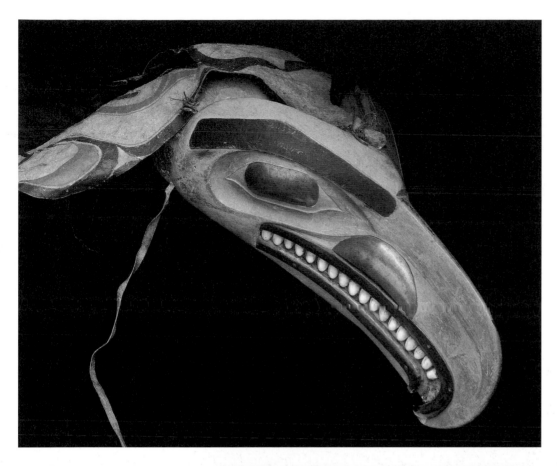

90
Heiltsuk, Artist Unknown
*Headdress Mask Representing
Eagle*, c. 1860
15.2 × 55.9 × 116.8
wood, copper, hide, opercula and paint
National Museum of Natural History,
Smithsonian Institution, Washington,
20571
Photo by Trevor Mills, Vancouver Art Gallery

91
Heiltsuk, Artist Unknown
Cannibal Bird Mask, c. 1870
72.3 × 58.4 × 137.1
wood, bear fur, cord and paint
American Museum of Natural History, New
York, 16/963
Photo by Trevor Mills, Vancouver Art Gallery

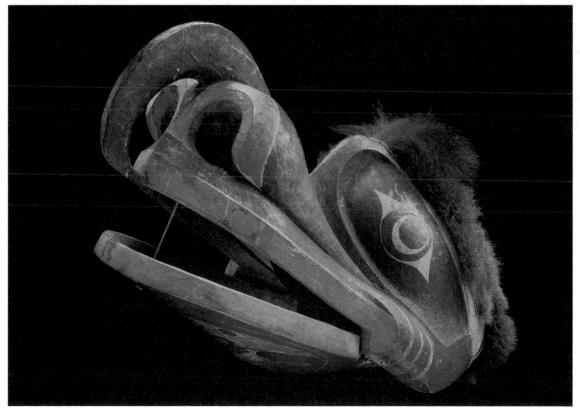

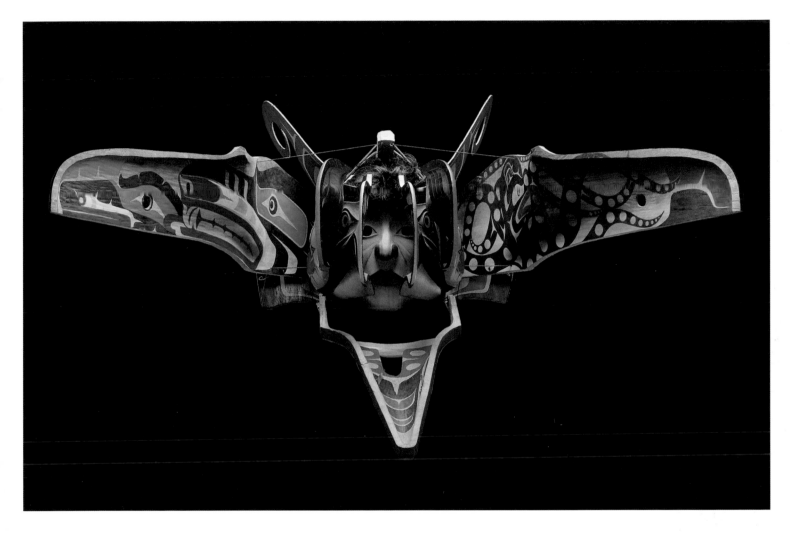

92 (facing page)
Kwakwa̱ka'wakw, Beau Dick
Mask Featuring Four Cannibal Birds, c. 1985
81.0 × 44.0 × 105.5
red cedar, yellow cedar, cedar bark, nails,
twine, leather and paint
Private Collection
Photo by Trevor Mills, Vancouver Art Gallery

93
Kwakwa̱ka'wakw, Stan Wamiss
(open view)
Triple Transformation Mask, 1997
50.5 × 61.0 × 97.5
red cedar, veneer, plywood, hair, hinges, twine
and paint
Private Collection
Photo by Trevor Mills, Vancouver Art Gallery

94
Haida, Guujaaw
Mask Representing Raven, 1980
20.0 × 77.0 × 18.5
red cedar, cedar bark, cloth, cedar branches,
feathers, leather, nails, nylon twine and paint
Private Collection
Photo by Trevor Mills, Vancouver Art Gallery

95 (facing page)
Kwakwaka'wakw, Tony Hunt
Mask Representing Huxwhukw,
1980
38.0 × 29.0 × 180.0
red cedar, cedar bark, brass nails, nylon twine
and leather
Private Collection
Photo by Trevor Mills, Vancouver Art Gallery

96 (facing page)
Heiltsuk, Artist Unknown
*Mask Representing Personified
Moon*, c. 1850
31.7 × 58.4 × 66.0
wood, pigment, hide, abalone shell and paint
American Museum of Natural History, New
York, 16/594
Photo by Trevor Mills, Vancouver Art Gallery

97
Kwakwa̱ka'wakw, Calvin Hunt
*Mask Representing Moon and
Eagle*, 1993
67.0 × 65.5 × 22.0
red cedar, copper, abalone shell, screws, nails
and paint
Private Collection
Photo by Trevor Mills, Vancouver Art Gallery

98
Haida, Reg Davidson
*Mask Representing Raven and
Dogfish*, c. 1990
50.0 × 21.0 × 25.0
red cedar, cedar bark, opercula, nails, twine
and paint
Private Collection
Photo by Trevor Mills, Vancouver Art Gallery

99 (facing page)
Nuxalk, Glenn Tallio
Mask Representing Thunder, 1990
30.0 × 24.0 × 24.5
red cedar, cedar bark, spruce root, baleen
and paint
Private Collection
Photo by Trevor Mills, Vancouver Art Gallery

100 (facing page)
Kwakw<u>aka</u>'wakw, Kevin Cranmer
Forehead Mask Representing <u>K</u>ulus,
1992
29.5 × 22.0 × 68.0
red cedar, leather, nails, rabbit fur, feathers,
cloth, nylon twine and paint
Private Collection
Photo by Trevor Mills, Vancouver Art Gallery

101
Kwakw<u>aka</u>'wakw, Richard Hunt
Mask Representing Ancestral Sun,
1978
50.5 × 58.0 × 20.0
red cedar, nylon twine, screws and paint
Private Collection
Photo by Trevor Mills, Vancouver Art Gallery

102
Haida, Robert Davidson
Mask Representing Eagle Spirit,
1980
22.8 × 22.3 × 15.5
red cedar, maple, hide, feathers, brass, leather,
opercula and paint
Private Collection
Photo by Trevor Mills, Vancouver Art Gallery

103 (facing page)
Nisga'a, Norman Tait
Mask Representing Moon, 1983
19.6 × 21.7 × 7.0
wood and paint
Royal Ontario Museum, Toronto, 983.120.1
Photo courtesy Royal Ontario Museum

THE UNDERSEA WORLD

The Undersea World is equal in mystery and power to that of the Sky, although there are more malevolent beings in the watery deep (Figures 104 to 114). In some cases, undersea creatures have counterparts in the other domains: Sea Eagles, Sea Ravens, Sea Bears and Sea Wolves are separate entities which are ocean-bound. In a Nuu-chah-nulth example, this parallel existence goes beyond equivalency; for them, wolves and killer whales share a single persona. There are Nuu-chah-nulth people who have, within living memory, witnessed a pod of killer whales disappear into a sandy spit only to emerge as wolves on the other side. Names and tangible privileges reflecting this duality are among the most honoured that a Nuu-chah-nulth person could expect to receive during a lifetime.

All Northwest Coast groups incorporate a belief that an undersea power controls much of that domain, but their concepts are by no means the same. The Kwakwaka'wakw call their sea chief Ḵumugwe', and he lives in a fabulous house made of copper planks and roof boards. He commands the lives of the significant sea creatures— whales, killer whales, sea lions, salmon and herring. Some of these are his servants and attend his every need, although they can, when appropriate, disappear to their ancestral homes in the distant west. His visage is usually stern, with perhaps an air of benevolence (Figure 104). His name translates variously as Copper Maker or Wealthy, and he is indeed the source of copper for the mortal world, bestowing it and other powers upon those whom he favours. He travels about in a copper canoe which moves without any apparent means of propulsion.

More fearsome are the sea monsters which threaten seafaring folk. These can cause sudden squalls and tide rips, emerge unexpectedly as reefs, or overturn canoes and swallow the occupants whole. Masks representing these sea monsters are often adorned with copper, reflecting the wealth of their deep-water origins (Figure 106). Some beings are always dangerous, while others are ultimately friendly, emerging from the depths to become founding ancestors. One such is 'Namxxelagiyu (Figure 105), who occupied the waters at the mouth of the Nimpkish River. From its forehead grew a glowing crystal which, when struck by the harpoon of an ancestral hero, caused the hunter to fall down in a swoon. When he revived, his weapon pulsated with a power that enabled him to kill prey at will or turn enemies into stone by simply pointing his harpoon at them.

Another representation of the same creature (Figure 107) depicts the monster as a halibutlike fish, with a man standing on its back. When the world was young, this fish creature emerged from the water at the mouth of the Nimpkish River and transformed to become the man standing on its back. In this form, he began to build a house which he could complete only with the assistance of a Thunderbird. Together, the two became the founders of the 'Namgis tribe.

104
Kwakwaka'wakw, Artist
Unknown
Mask Representing Ḵumugwe',
c. 1880
48.9 × 43.2 × 15.2
alder, red cedar bark, cloth and paint
Seattle Art Museum, Gift of John H. Hauberg,
Seattle, 91.1.30
Photo by Paul Macapia, courtesy Seattle Art
Museum

105
Kwakw<u>a</u>ka'wakw, Tony Hunt Jr.
*Mask Representing 'N<u>a</u>mgis
Ancestor*, 1987
69.0 × 60.0 × 27.0
red cedar, copper, nylon twine, maple, crystal
and paint
Royal British Columbia Museum, Victoria,
18651
Photo courtesy Royal British Columbia Museum

106
Kwakw<u>a</u>ka'wakw, Henry Hunt
Mask Representing Sea Monster,
1970
31.6 × 28.7 × 20.7
red cedar, copper and paint
Royal British Columbia Museum, Victoria,
13215
Photo by Trevor Mills, Vancouver Art Gallery

107 (facing page)
Kwakw<u>a</u>ka'wakw, Joe Wilson
*Mask Representing 'N<u>a</u>mgis
Ancestor*, 1998
77.0 × 45.0 × 34.0
red cedar, cedar bark, cloth, nylon twine,
hemlock branches, shell beads, metal bells
and paint
Campbell River Museum, Campbell River, no
accession number
Photo by Trevor Mills, Vancouver Art Gallery

108
Kwakwaka'wakw, Richard Hunt
Mask Representing Killer Whale,
1978
58.0 × 60.0 × 1925.0
red cedar, nylon twine, leather, nails and paint
Royal British Columbia Museum, Victoria,
16460
Photo by Trevor Mills, Vancouver Art Gallery

Killer Whales (also called orcas) are found in north Pacific waters, and they may emerge as ancestors (Figure 108). Their role among the Nuu-chah-nulth has already been described. The Kwakwaka'wakw respect Killer Whales because they view them as reincarnations of deceased chiefs. Orcas have been known to arrive on prescribed dates in front of certain villages, where they are welcomed honorifically. It is unwise to threaten them in any way, and attempts to kill or injure them always result in misfortune for the attacker. The Nisga'a cast tobacco on the waters, in a gesture of good will, when Killer Whales approach.

The Haida view important sea creatures as races of people who operate in the underwater realm much as human society does on land. The Killer Whale people (Figure 109) are the most dominant and the most feared. In many cases, their villages are contiguous with both the real and mythic Haida towns. Malevolent Killer Whales can transform into reefs, the stone-bound fins of which can only be detected at low tide. Despite their uncharitable nature, the orcas which transformed into reefs became highly regarded crests for the appropriate lineage.

The Haida view of the Killer Whale is summarized in the following tale: "Once, a man in his canoe passed near a Killer Whale and struck its fin with a stone. The following morning, smoke was seen rising from a nearby point, and he and his companions went to see who was there. When they got near, they saw a man mending his canoe, which had a break in the side. The man called out to him, saying, 'Why did you break my canoe?' From that they knew that Killer Whales are really the canoes of Ocean-People."[35]

A benign and harmless Kwakwaka'wakw creature of the Undersea World is the Bagwis, characterized by prominent incisor teeth which frequently causes this mask to be mistakenly identified as a beaver. Bagwis likes to play around kelp beds and is curious but shy in the presence of humans. These masks may stand alone or be shown with a bird, usually a loon, attached to the forehead.

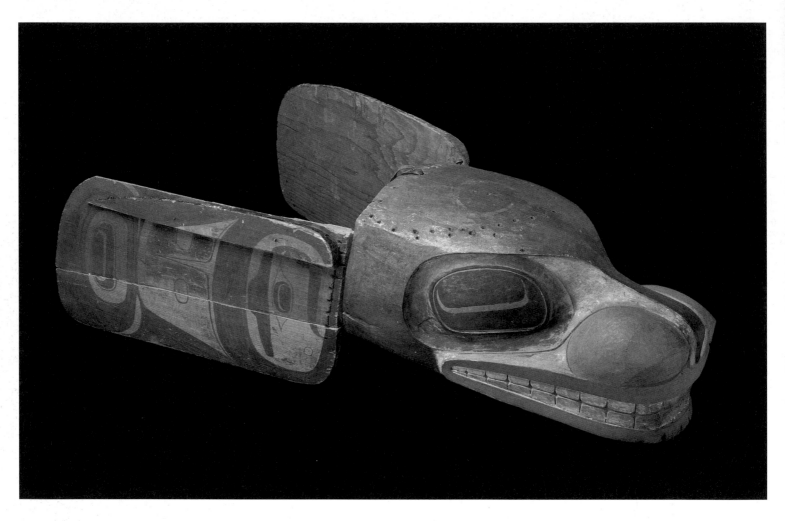

109
Haida, Artist Unknown
Mask Representing Killer Whale,
19th century
20.3 × 20.3 × 73.7
wood and paint
National Museum of Natural History,
Smithsonian Institution, Washington, 89102
Photo by Trevor Mills, Vancouver Art Gallery

110 (facing page)
Haida, Robert Davidson
Mask Representing Shark, 1986
82.0 × 57.5 × 38.0
red cedar, copper, horsehair, opercula, abalone
shell, leather, aluminum, yew and paint
Private Collection
Photo by Trevor Mills, Vancouver Art Gallery

111 (facing page)
Tsimshian, Artist Unknown
Forehead Mask Representing Sea Lion, c. 1870
22.0 × 49.0 × 40
wood, opercula and paint
Royal Ontario Museum, Toronto, 926.34.3
Photo courtesy Royal Ontario Museum

112
Kwakwaka'wakw, Wayne Alfred
(open view)
Mask Representing Transformation Salmon, 1992
43.0 × 121.0 × 43.0
red cedar, cedar bark, cloth, nylon twine, nails, hinges and paint
Private Collection
Photo by Trevor Mills, Vancouver Art Gallery

113
Kwakwaka'wakw, Wayne Alfred
*Mask Representing Raven Fin
Killer Whale*, 1992
61.0 × 33.0 × 152.5
red cedar, cedar bark, nylon twine, leather,
nails and paint
Private Collection
Photo by Trevor Mills, Vancouver Art Gallery

114 (facing page)
Gitxsan, Walter Harris
*Headdress Representing Killer
Whale*, 1969
49.8 × 66.0 × 116.0
birch, hair, twine, copper and paint
Royal British Columbia Museum, Victoria
13920
Photo by Trevor Mills, Vancouver Art Gallery

THE MORTAL WORLD

The Mortal World today is very different from the one that existed in mythic times. When the world was young, the myth people occupied our world and interacted in it just as humans do (Figures 115 and 142). The one constant is the landscape: place names, hundreds of which have been recorded for all Northwest Coast groups, reflect both a past age and the present. In the Mortal World are the creatures normally associated with the land as well as some supernatural beings. It is a realm occupied by both real and mythic creatures. Early in time, the myth people were threatened by a flood of epic proportions that covered the known world. The ancients devised various ways to survive: they tethered their largest canoes to the highest mountain tops, they constructed catamarans on whose decks they built shelters, they plugged all the cracks in their houses and waited inside for the flood waters to retreat. When the waters subsided, the myth people underwent a final metamorphosis and became the biological progenitors of humankind. But they did not forget their animal incarnations and the specific locales where they first transformed into humans.

Familiar creatures in this realm include certain birds such as the Sandhill Crane (Figure 116) the Puffin (Figure 117). The former, while familiar, appears here in its supernatural form. According to the story, a hero waited for a low tide to reveal a hole in a rock, through which he entered the Undersea World and approached the house of Copper Maker. A Crane that stood guard outside warned his chief of the visitor's arrival. Copper Maker bestowed his name on the visitor and sent him back to the Mortal World with the bird as his treasure, hence the right of his descendants to use the Sandhill Crane mask. This particular example was made in the 1950s by Kwakwaka'wakw carver Mungo Martin;[36] Figure 115 shows a recent one from the hand of George Hunt Jr., who chose to represent the bird as a Great Blue Heron.

Wolves are also significant ancestors for most Northwest Coast tribes (Figures 4, 24, 119, 125, 126 and 128). They are central to the Nuu-chah-nulth *tlōkwāna*, commonly called the Wolf ritual, and serve to capture initiates and instruct them in the ways of the ceremony before returning them to the Mortal World. Certain Nuu-chah-nulth families have the right to use as many as forty such masks at one time.

The grizzly bear in both natural and supernatural form also dominates the myth histories of all Northwest Coast groups. Northern peoples recount versions of the Bear Mother myth in which a young mortal woman is captured by a Grizzly Bear, marries him, and produces half-human, half-grizzly cubs. In time, she is rescued by her hunter brother. Variations of this story also are rendered on totem poles and in crest art.

The history of the Grizzly Bear mask (Figure 5) was recounted by its owner, Chief Mungo Martin, when he placed it in a museum collection prior to his death in 1963.

115
Kwakwaka'wakw, George Hunt Jr.
Mask Representing Heron and Ḵumugwe', 1990
103.0 × 150.0 × 104.0
red cedar, yellow cedar, horsehair, cedar bark, rope, nylon twine, canvas, copper, abalone shell, screws, nails, feathers and paint
Pegasus Gallery, Salt Spring Island
Photo by Trevor Mills, Vancouver Art Gallery

116 (facing page)
Kwakw<u>aka</u>'wakw, Mungo Martin
*Mask Representing Supernatural
Sandhill Crane*, c. 1956
102.0 × 157.0 × 42.5
red cedar, cotton twine, nails and paint
Royal British Columbia Museum, Victoria,
9250
Photo by Trevor Mills, Vancouver Art Gallery

117
Haida, Artist Unknown
Mask Representing Puffin, c. 1860
27.0 × 21.5 × 55.5
wood and paint
McCord Museum of Canadian History,
Montréal, ME 892.20
Photo courtesy Musée McCord Museum

He dated the mask to about 1840 and recorded the name and tribal affiliation of its first owner, the occasion and location where it was first used, including the name of the host of the Potlatch and those of his participating family members, the names of the attending tribes, the name of the ceremonial house where it was first danced, and some of the other dances performed by guests at the event. Elegant and understated, this ancient Bear mask consists of an armature of red cedar wood, over which a pelt of grizzly bear fur has been stretched and pegged. A prized piece of brown bottle glass serves as an eye, outlined in vermilion. The nostrils and lips have been overpainted in recent times with enamel.[37]

To the Kwakw<u>aka</u>'wakw people, Dzunu<u>k</u>wa is a land-based creature who retained her mythic form after the great flood. She is a female giant, twice the height of a normal person, with a black hairy body and pendulous breasts. Her sleepy, sunken eyes are deep-set in her skull and what can be seen of them glows like coals. Her lips are pursed to indicate her cry, "Uu, huu, uu, uu" (Figure 6). On her back, she carries a basket in which she places human children she has captured, intending to eat them; but they manage to outwit her by luring her to their home village, where she is dispatched by a warrior. Masks representing her in this persona are large, nearly 60 centimetres (two feet) in height and are worn with a bearskin costume (Figure 120). Another variation of this mask is smaller, just large enough to fit over a human face, and is worn by a chief at the end of his Potlatch when his orator is summarizing his accomplishments. Archaic

118
Kwakwa̱ka'wakw, Artist
Unknown
Mask Representing Sea Lion, 19th
century
34.9 × 21.6 × 28.6
red cedar, sea lion whiskers and paint
University of Pennsylvania Museum of
Archaeology and Anthropology, Philadelphia,
29-175-34
Photo courtesy University of Pennsylvania
Museum

119 (facing page)
Gitx̱san, Earl Muldoe
Forehead Mask Representing Wolf,
1969
19.6 × 19.1 × 41.8
birch, horsehair, leather, copper, bone and
paint
Royal British Columbia Museum, Victoria,
13917
Photo by Trevor Mills, Vancouver Art Gallery

examples of the latter consistently feature a horizontal crease between temple and cheek; a very few late nineteenth-century examples tend towards realism (Figure 122).

The creatures which figure in the Kwakwaka'wakw Atłakim dance (described in Robert Joseph's essay) emerge from one dimension and are ultimately manifest in another, the Mortal World, where they reveal themselves to humankind. This dance can include as many as forty masks representing both supernatural and real birds, fish, ghosts, many forest spirits and human persona. Of the latter type is a family group, consisting of a pregnant woman (Figure 9), her husband, a midwife and several children, two of which are often "born" on the dance floor. Other spirits represented in this set are the Long Life Bringer (Figure 121) and the Laugher (Figure 7), whose uncontrolled guffaws provide comic relief. Placing such spirits in a preconceived category is difficult, but in the recounting of the associated legend, the assemblage is defined as spirits who inhabit a supernatural as well as a mortal forest.

The masks used in the Naxnóx dances of the Tsimshian Peoples originate as powers in the Spirit World and manifest themselves as humans or animals. Figures 19, 55, 131 and 140 may be Naxnóx masks. The "Eagle Woman" mask (Figure 54) was replicated in a contemporary version (Figure 132) by Gitxsan artist Walter Harris.

The dance of the Nułamał (fool) is one of the most ancient of Kwakwaka'wakw traditions, suggesting that it originated with them even though it is known among the Nuxalk and Nuu-chah-nulth. Nułamał masks collected in the 1840s are leonine in form (Figures 124 and 129) and were probably inspired by the decorated cathead timber used on early sailing vessels to secure an anchor.[38] One outstanding characteristic of the creature is a large nose from which, it is said, mucus constantly drips. In late nineteenth-century examples, the nose is even more exaggerated (Figure 12). An interesting evolution takes place in certain masks, where the stylized whiskers of the muzzle (Figure 129) turn into profiles of hands laid along the cheeks (Figure 130).[39]

120 (facing page)
Kwakw<u>a</u>ka'wakw chiefs proudly
display their ceremonial regalia
for the Indian Land Commis-
sioners in Alert Bay, 1914. The
Dzunu<u>k</u>wa mask shown in
Figure 6 leans against the back
wall, with its full costume of
black bear fur attached. Artist
Chief Mungo Martin is standing to the left of the costume.
Photo courtesy Royal British Columbia
Museum, Victoria, PN2777

121
Kwakw<u>a</u>ka'wakw, Beau Dick
*Mask Representing Long Life
Bringer*, 1982
39.5 × 23.0 × 14.0
alder, cedar bark, twine, rubber and paint
Private Collection
Photo by Trevor Mills, Vancouver Art Gallery

147

122
Kwakwa̲ka'wakw, Bond Sound
Chief's Dzunu̲ḵwa Mask, c. 1890
27.4 × 23.0 × 25.5
hemlock, human hair, twine, baleen and paint
Royal British Columbia Museum, Victoria,
12924
Photo courtesy Royal British Columbia Museum

123 (facing page)
Kwakwa̲ka'wakw, Artist
Unknown
Mask Representing Dzunu̲ḵwa,
c. 1880
50.8 × 40.6 × 33.0
wood, hair, hide, nails and paint
Milwaukee Public Museum, Milwaukee, 17359
Photo by Trevor Mills, Vancouver Art Gallery

124 (facing page)
Kwakw_aka_'wakw, Artist Unknown
Mask Representing Nuḷ_a_maḷ,
c. 1840
35.5 × 22.5 × 15.0
wood and paint
Staatliche Museen zu Berlin—Preußischer
Kulturbesitz Museum für Völkerkunde, Berlin,
IV-A524
Photo courtesy Staatliche Museen zu Berlin

125
Kwakw_aka_'wakw*, Artist Unknown
Forehead Mask Representing Wolf,
c. 1860
48.2 × 48.2 × 92.7
wood, hair and paint
American Museum of Natural History,
New York, 16/384
Photo by Trevor Mills, Vancouver Art Gallery

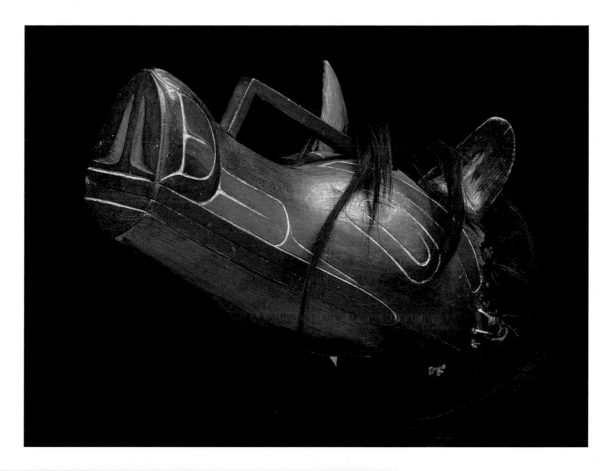

126
Kwakw_aka_'wakw, Artist Unknown
Forehead Mask Representing Wolf,
c. 1860
17.8 × 19.0 × 41.9
wood, hair, feathers, cedar bark and paint
National Museum of Natural History,
Smithsonian Institution, Washington,
274261
Photo by Trevor Mills, Vancouver Art Gallery

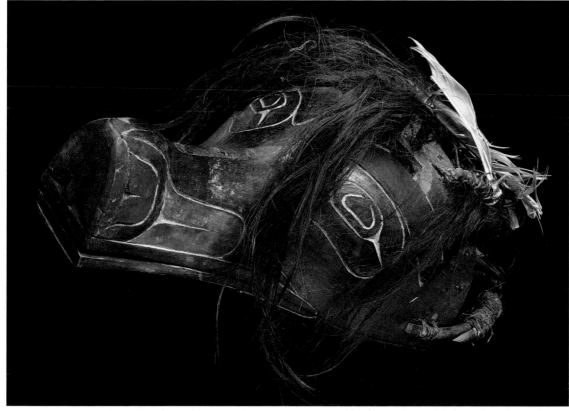

127 (facing page)
Kwakwaka'wakw, Joe Wilson
Mask Representing Chief's Dzunukwa, 1994
28.0 × 22.0 × 14.0
red cedar, horsehair, black bear fur, nails,
nylon twine, leather and paint
Private Collection
Photo by Trevor Mills, Vancouver Art Gallery

128
Tlingit, Artist Unknown
Forehead Mask Representing Wolf,
c. 1880
43.2 × 20.3 × 26.7
wood, hair, copper, opercula, cloth and paint
Portland Art Museum, Portland,
48.3.415
Photo by Eduardo Calderon

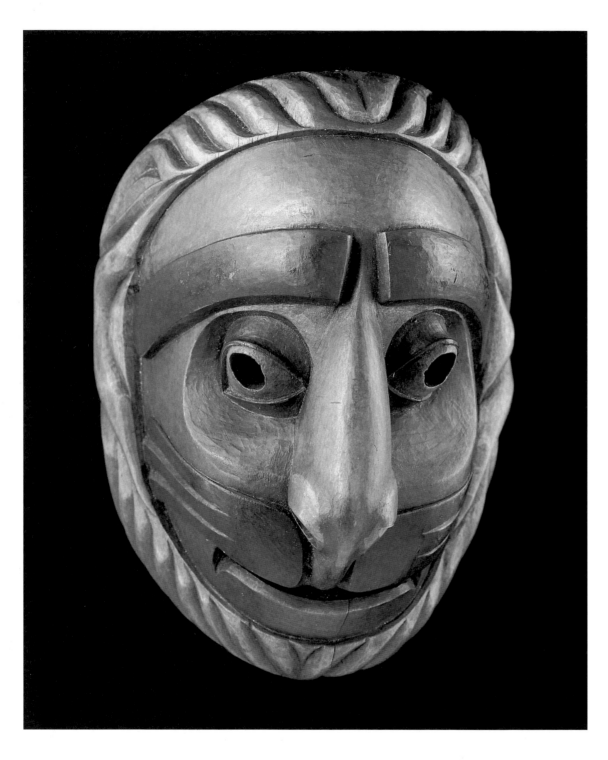

129
Kwakw<u>aka</u>'wakw, Artist
Unknown
Mask Representing Nuɫ<u>a</u>maɫ,
c. 1840
27.8 × 20.0 × 16.6
wood and paint
Royal British Columbia Museum, Victoria,
15981
Photo by Trevor Mills, Vancouver Art Gallery

130 (facing page)
Kwakw<u>aka</u>'wakw, Artist
Unknown
Mask Representing Nuɫ<u>a</u>maɫ,
c. 1870
36.0 × 23.0 × 13.5
wood and paint
Royal Ontario Museum, Toronto, HN 386
Photo courtesy Royal Ontario Museum

131
Nisga'a, Artist Unknown
Naxnóx Mask, 19th century
26.5 × 25.2 × 21.7
red cedar, copper, nails, fur and paint
Royal British Columbia Museum, Victoria,
14308
Photo by Trevor Mills, Vancouver Art Gallery

132 (facing page)
Gitxsan, Walter Harris
Mask Representing Eagle Woman,
1969
71.5 × 24.4 × 13.6
birch, hair, twine, cedar bark, copper and paint
Royal British Columbia Museum, Victoria,
13918
Photo by Trevor Mills, Vancouver Art Gallery

133 (facing page)
Kwakw<u>aka</u>'wakw, Tony Hunt Jr.
<u>X</u>wi<u>x</u>wi Mask, 1989
46.5 × 35.3 × 19.5
red cedar, cloth, cord, nails and paint
Royal British Columbia Museum, Victoria,
18983
Photo by Trevor Mills, Vancouver Art Gallery

134
Kwakw<u>aka</u>'wakw, Tony Hunt Jr.
<u>X</u>wi<u>x</u>wi Mask, 1989
50.5 × 42.5 × 19.5
red cedar, cloth, cord, nails and paint
Royal British Columbia Museum, Victoria
18984
Photo by Trevor Mills, Vancouver Art Gallery

The Coast Salish have only one type of mask and associated costume, which together are called the Sxwaixwe, used to cleanse and protect individuals of noble rank. The term Sxwaixwe is so archaic that a translation is not possible. By mid-nineteenth century, the rights to the Sxwaixwe mask and dance had been acquired by both Kwakw<u>aka</u>'wakw and Nuu-chah-nulth families, who reduced the pronunciation to <u>X</u>wi<u>x</u>wi. The two Nuu-chah-nulth masks in Figures 137 and 138 represent a somewhat minimal rendering; late nineteenth-century Kwakwaka'wakw versions were elaborately carved and painted. In the 1920s, some Kwakw<u>aka</u>'wakw artists introduced simpler masks dominated by a painted white ground (Figures 135 and 136). More recently, Tony Hunt Jr. produced an exceptional contemporary pair (Figures 133 and 134) based on the late nineteenth-century type.

135 (facing page)
Kwakw<u>a</u>ka'wakw, Willie Seaweed
<u>X</u>wi<u>x</u>wi Mask, c. 1930
22.8 × 17.7 × 34.2
red cedar and paint
University of British Columbia, Museum of
Anthropology, Vancouver, A3662
Photo by Trevor Mills, Vancouver Art Gallery

136
Kwakw<u>a</u>ka'wakw, Willie Seaweed
<u>X</u>wi<u>x</u>wi Mask, c. 1930
24.7 × 15.2 × 33.0
red cedar and paint
University of British Columbia, Museum of
Anthropology, Vancouver, A4095
Photo by Trevor Mills, Vancouver Art Gallery

137
Nuu-chah-nulth, Artist
Unknown
<u>Xwixwi</u> Mask, late 19th century
55.9 × 40.6 × 25.4
wood and paint
University of Pennsylvania Museum of
Archaeology and Anthropology, Philadelphia,
29-175-31
Photo courtesy University of Pennsylvania
Museum

138
Nuu-chah-nulth, Artist
Unknown
Xwixwi Mask, late 19th century
46.4 × 42.8 × 25.4
wood and paint
University of Pennsylvania Museum of
Archaeology and Anthropology, Philadelphia,
29-175-29
Photo courtesy University of Pennsylvania
Museum

139
Nuu-chah-nulth, Art
Thompson
Mask Representing Warrior, 1989
63.0 × 23.5 × 25.0
red cedar, alder, cedar bark, horsehair, leather,
nails, twine, copper and paint
Spirit Wrestler Gallery, Vancouver
Photo by Trevor Mills, Vancouver Art Gallery

140 (facing page)
Nisga'a, Artist Unknown
*Naxnóx Mask Representing
Skimsim*, 19th century
29.7 × 26.7 × 33.6
cedar, nails, paint, red cedar and bark
Royal British Columbia Museum, Victoria,
1505
Photo by Trevor Mills, Vancouver Art Gallery

141
Nuu-chah-nulth, Ron
Hamilton
*Mask Representing Ch'ihaa
(Ancestor)*, c. 1970
23.0 × 16.5 × 18.0
alder and paint
Private Collection
Photo by Trevor Mills, Vancouver Art Gallery

142 (facing page)
Nuxalk, Artist Unknown
*Mask Representing Spirit
Creature*, c. 1880
30.5 × 20.3 × 21.6
alder, cedar bark, hair, cloth, twine, nails
and paint
Seattle Art Museum, Gift of John H.
Hauberg, Seattle, 91.1.34
Photo by Paul Macapia, courtesy Seattle Art
Museum

THE SPIRIT WORLD

The Spirit World cannot be fixed in a single or particular space, and opinions as to its locale vary as much within a single tribal group as it does between them (Figures 143 to 153). Some say that it exists far beyond the western horizon and may only be reached by following an undersea route. Others say it is underground, usually accessed through a graveyard or by entering a coffin which proves to be a doorway to the underworld. Or it can be the Milky Way, down which the soul spirals to oblivion. Perhaps it is best viewed as coexisting with the Mortal World, separated from it only by a thin veil which few can penetrate. Those on the other side can access the Mortal World with ease and at will.

Ghosts can be manifestations of dear departed relatives who occasionally return through the veil to visit the Mortal World. When death approaches, they gather in a group to conduct the dying person to a better land. Other apparitions have a darker character.

One malevolent ghostly spirit is universally recognized—under different guises—by all Northwest Coast groups. His characteristics are constant: he is the keeper of drowned souls; he causes loss of reason and sanity; he lures those seeking escape into the night woods with faint firelight. His victims survive by finding minimal sustenance on the forest floor or in the intertidal region.

Among the Kwakwaka'wakw, this ghostly spirit is known as B̲ak̕w̲a̲s, or "man of the ground embodiment."[40] Although diminutive, he can leap through the woods with strides four times longer than those of an average man. He has a green, hairy body, is nominally shy, and has a frightening, skeletal visage (Figures 3, 143 and 145). The souls of those who drown or who are enticed to eat his food are lost forever and become members of his ghostly retinue. Occasionally, those whom B̲ak̕w̲a̲s captures can be saved, but only by subduing them with menstrual blood.

His counterpart among the Heiltsuk and Nuu-chah-nulth is very similar. In Nuu-chah-nulth territory, those who nearly drown reach a beach in an exhausted state and revive to the point of being able to follow his pale, ever-moving fire deeper and deeper into the woods. In time, they become as cold as ice, their bodies turn deathly white, and their faces assume a skeletal quality as the Makah version (Figure 144) indicates.

Among the Haida, those who barely escape drowning are similarly attracted to an elusive light. If they reach the fire, they lose all reason and become a *gagiit*.[41] Near starvation, they end up living in the intertidal zone, searching for what food they can catch by hand, usually small spiny fish and sea urchins. Because they do not have utensils, they consume their minimal diet raw, and the bones and spines of their prey become embedded permanently in their lips (Figures 148 and 149). In his representation of a gagiit (Figure 146), one of only two masks known to have been carved by him, the Haida master Charles Edenshaw chose not to insert spines. Edenshaw's descendant Robert Davidson

143
Kwakw̲a̲ka'wakw, Artist Unknown
Mask Representing B̲ak̕w̲a̲s,
c. 1880
37.1 × 27.0 × 20.4
red cedar, horsehair, nails and paint
Royal British Columbia Museum, Victoria, 1913
Photo courtesy Royal British Columbia Museum

144
Makah, Greg Colfax
Mask Representing Pukubts, 1990
30.5 × 21.6 × 20.5
alder, cedar bark, horsetail, red cloth, graphite
and paint
Legacy Gallery, Seattle
Photo by Trevor Mills, Vancouver Art Gallery

145 (facing page)
Kwakwaka'wakw, Mervyn Child
Mask Representing Baḱwas, 1985
30.0 × 34.0 × 21.0
red cedar, horsehair, cloth, nails, nylon twine
and paint
Private Collection
Photo by Trevor Mills, Vancouver Art Gallery

146 (facing page)
Haida, Charles Edenshaw
Mask Representing Gagiit, c. 1905
53.3 × 76.2
wood, hair, string and paint
American Museum of Natural History, New
York, 16.1/128
Photo by Trevor Mills, Vancouver Art Gallery

147
Haida, Robert Davidson
Mask Representing Gagiit, 1983
34.0 × 37.5 × 24.0
red cedar, horsehair, screws, cloth and paint
Private Collection
Photo by Trevor Mills, Vancouver Art Gallery

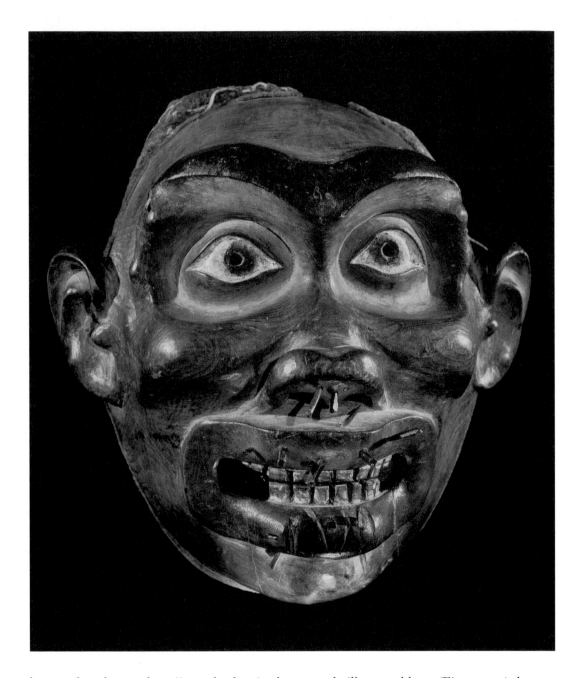

148
Haida, Artist Unknown
Mask Representing Gagiit,
c. 1860
25.7 × 25.0 × 15.6
wood and paint
Royal British Columbia Museum, Victoria,
18653
Photo courtesy Royal British Columbia
Museum

149 (facing page)
Haida, Reg Davidson
Mask Representing Gagiit, c. 1988
31.0 × 33.5 × 24.0
red cedar, horsehair, opercula and paint
Private Collection
Photo by Trevor Mills, Vancouver Art Gallery

has produced several gagiit masks, but in the example illustrated here (Figure 147), he too has opted to eliminate the spines. Moving about on their hands and knees as they do, gagiit eventually assume the form of land otters, their bodies covered with a dense pelage.

The Tlingit equivalent is the Land Otter, which they fear more than any other creature. It is the most powerful supernatural force in their universe and only shamans can successfully overpower it. The Land Otter uses guile to cause the unsuspecting traveller's canoe to capsize, thus acquiring the soul of the deceased. It is featured in various shaman's paraphernalia, including masks.

150 (facing page)
Haida, Artist Unknown
*Mask Representing Supernatural
Being*, collected 1879
25.5 × 19.0
wood, copper, hair, hide and paint
Canadian Museum of Civilization, Hull,
VII-B-10
Photo courtesy Canadian Museum of
Civilization, s92-4164

151
Tlingit, Artist Unknown
Headdress Mask, c. 1850
8.8 × 22.8 × 26.1
wood and paint
American Museum of Natural History, New
York, E/1376
Photo by Trevor Mills, Vancouver Art Gallery

One of the functions of the Tlingit shaman was to act as a mediator between the Mortal World and those often malevolent forces originating in the ghostland. He employed the spirits of the deceased to help cure the sick, foretell the future and divine events occurring at a considerable distance. His spirit helpers, represented by both humanoid masks (Figure 151) and anthropmorphic masks (Figure 152), assisted in the curing rituals.

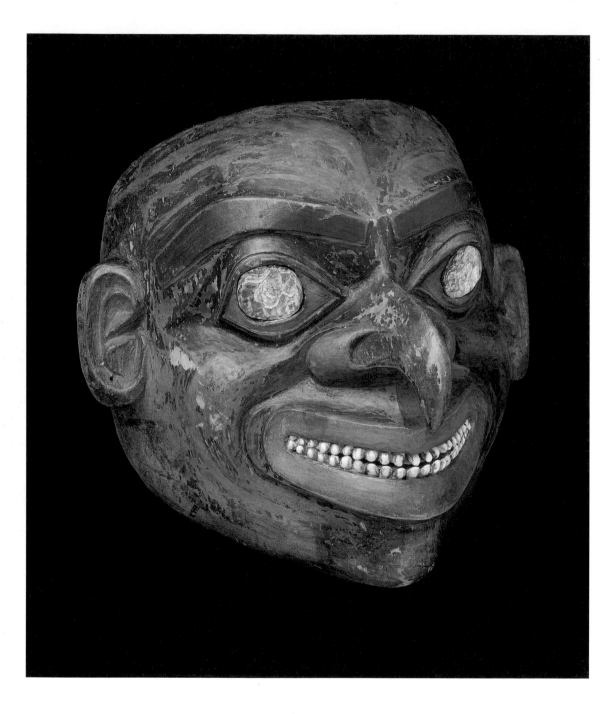

152
Tlingit, Artist Unknown
*Mask Representing Humanoid
Eagle*, c. 1840
38.1 × 57.1 × 62.2
wood, pigment, opercula and abalone shell
American Museum of Natural History, New
York, 19/852
Photo by Trevor Mills, Vancouver Art Gallery

153 (facing page)
Tlingit, Artist Unknown
Mask, 19th century
25.4 × 21.6 × 11.4
wood, hair, opercula, brass coins and paint
National Museum of Natural History,
Smithsonian Institution, Washington, 76855
Photo by Trevor Mills, Vancouver Art Gallery

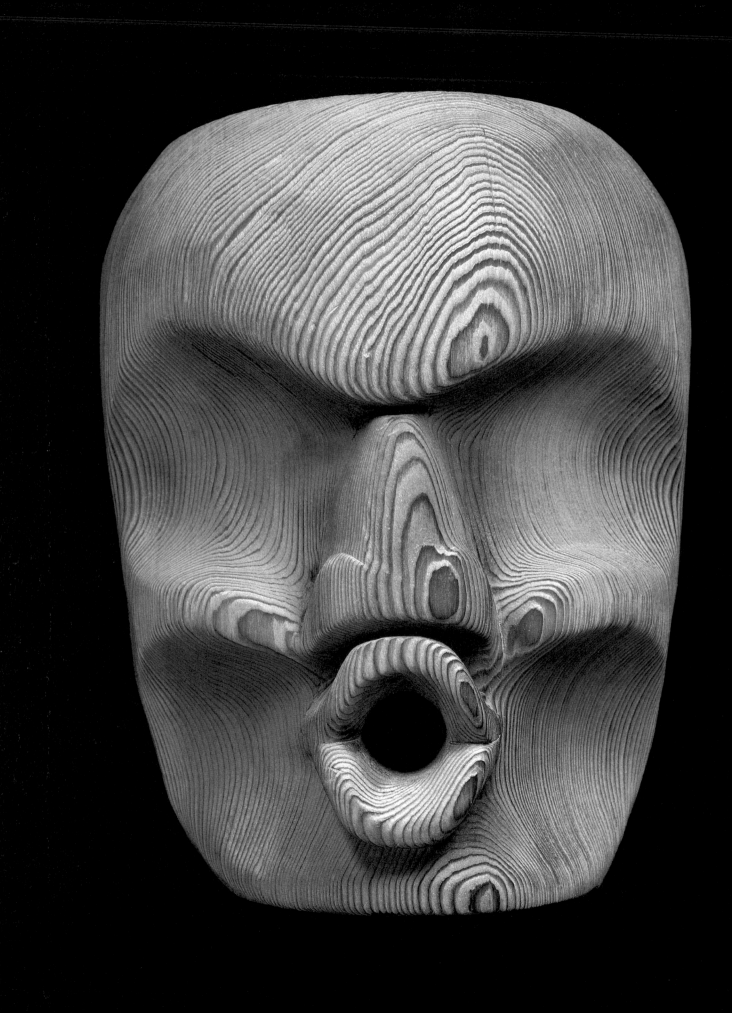

ENDURING AND EVOLVING TRADITIONS

Northwest Coast artistic traditions are always evolving, as curator Steven C. Brown has pointed out,[42] though certain conventions and subjects must survive in order to define a continuum. One such example involves the celebrated cannibal bird masks that originated on the central coast; within a century, they moved from understated representations (Figure 84) to flamboyant expressions that are so elaborate they can be described as baroque (Figure 87).

Another example is the Kaigani Haida labret-woman mask (Figure 38) made for sale in the early 1820s, which possibly had its genesis in the Tlingit shaman's mask and continued in its commercial manifestation through later variations (Figure 34), effectively culminating in a subtype created by Massett master carvers in the 1870s (Figure 46). Contemporary variants have recently been introduced (Figures 155 and 156). This type of mask is one of many such artistic dialogues which span nearly two centuries.

Kwakwaka'wakw artist and chief Mungo Martin moved to Victoria in 1952 to carve replica and original totem poles for the British Columbia Provincial Museum (now the Royal British Columbia Museum). In his spare time, he carved masks and model poles, much as his stepfather and artistic mentor Charlie James had done decades earlier (Figure 73). The commercial outlet which Martin supplied discovered that his brightly enamel-painted masks did not sell easily, and the proprietor convinced him to provide unpainted red cedar masks (Figure 157), which proved to be much more marketable. Martin's apprentice Henry Hunt continued this tradition, creating handsome, intricately carved works that were not painted and emphasized the grain of the wood. In later years, Henry's son Tony Hunt used a matte-finish paint to colour some details while leaving the primary ground in its natural cedar finish (Figure 68).

Ellen Neel (1916–1966), a granddaughter of the aforementioned Charlie James, was the only woman carver of note during her lifetime. In her adult years, she lived and worked in Vancouver, where she experienced marketing challenges similar to those Mungo Martin faced in Victoria. Her solution was to rough out a mask, wire-brush it to expose the grain, then scorch it with flame as a finishing touch (Figure 154).[43]

It is both ironic and fitting that the newest mask featured in the exhibition (but not shown here) is an ancestor mask made by Makah artist Greg Colfax of Neah Bay. This Grandmother mask was commissioned by the granddaughter of a missionary couple who had served native communities on the Olympic Peninsula of Washington state in the early twentieth century. This link from today to the early nineteenth-century human face masks which were made for trade to King George and Boston men exemplifies the ingenuity and wit of Northwest Coast cultures and the enduring strength of their artistic traditions.

154
Kwakwaka'wakw, Ellen Neel
Mask Representing Dzunukwa,
c. 1955
24.0 × 19.0 × 15.5
red cedar
Private Collection
Photo by Trevor Mills, Vancouver Art Gallery

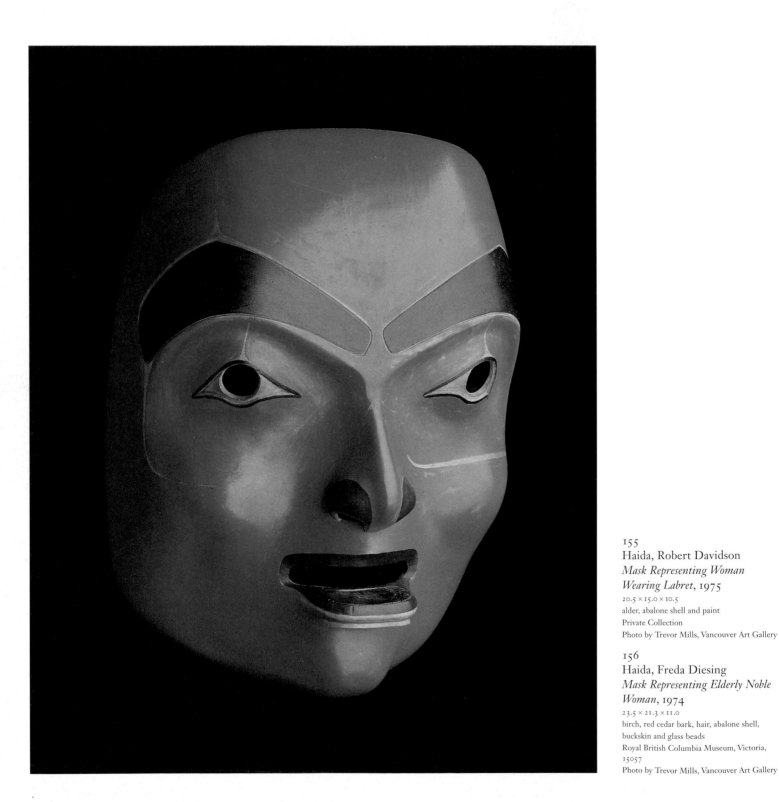

155
Haida, Robert Davidson
*Mask Representing Woman
Wearing Labret*, 1975
20.5 × 15.0 × 10.5
alder, abalone shell and paint
Private Collection
Photo by Trevor Mills, Vancouver Art Gallery

156
Haida, Freda Diesing
*Mask Representing Elderly Noble
Woman*, 1974
23.5 × 21.3 × 11.0
birch, red cedar bark, hair, abalone shell,
buckskin and glass beads
Royal British Columbia Museum, Victoria,
15057
Photo by Trevor Mills, Vancouver Art Gallery

Contemporary Northwest Coast artists are not only inspired to create masks with meaning for both sale and ceremonial use but many of them also are committed to passing on their cultural and artistic traditions, with deep roots that predate the memories of seven generations. Many coastal groups teach their young people that they must consider the impact of their lives and actions on the future—looking seven generations to the morrow to ensure that their cultures will be alive and strong for posterity.

157
Kwakw<u>aka</u>'wakw, Mungo Martin
Mask Representing Echo, c. 1955
30.9 × 29.9 × 35.0
red cedar
Royal British Columbia Museum, Victoria,
16512
Photo by Trevor Mills, Vancouver Art Gallery

NOTES

1
Tsimshian Peoples is a collective term that includes four linguistically related groups which inhabit the Nass and Skeena River drainages and the mainland coast south to Princess Royal Island.

2
Kwakwaka'wakw artist Charlie George of Blunden Harbour, personal communication to the author.

3
Samuel A. Barrett, field notes, Bancroft Library, University of California, Berkeley.

4
The two Nuu-chah-nulth masks in Figures 27 and 31 are typical examples from this era. Minimal and understated, they reflect a conservative, archaic style which appears to have a time depth of more than 1500 years.

5
J. C. H. King, *Artificial Curiosities from the Northwest Coast of America*, 21.

6
The East India Marine Society purpose statement, in the pamphlet *The East India Marine Associates* (n.p., n.d.) in the Peabody Essex Museum, Salem, Massachusetts.

7
William Fraser Tolmie, *Physician and Fur Trader: The Journals of William Fraser Tolmie*, 327.

8
Tolmie, *Physician and Fur Trader*, 333.

9
Tolmie, *Physician and Fur Trader*, 294-97.

10
The Naxnóx (spirit) is a representation of a hereditary name. The performer wearing a Naxnóx mask becomes a manifestation of an ancestor or other spirit power reflected in that name.

11
Haida oral histories suggest there was a migration in the seventeenth century from Haida Gwaii (the Queen Charlotte Islands) to the Prince of Wales Archipelago in what is now southeastern Alaska. This Alaskan branch is known as the Kaigani Haida, a name derived from the village of Kaigani which was a major calling place during the days of the sea-otter trade.

12
Presumably the latitude reading refers to the location of Fort Simpson, which lies three or four nautical miles north of that bearing. The inscription indicating that the masks represent a "tribe near Fort Simpson" reinforces the Kaigani attribution. Tolmie, who was a conduit for Haida and other northern coast artifacts, mentions having contact with various "Kygarnie Indians."

13
Where we considered it appropriate, we have reattributed the masks, illustrated here, that were collected by Israel Powell.

14
Bill Holm, *Spirit and Ancestor: A Century of Northwest Coast Indian Art at the Burke Museum*, 232.

15
Proceedings of the Massachusetts Historical Society, Vol. 1, October 1794, 76-77.

16
George T. Emmons and Frederica de Laguna, *The Tlingit Indians*, 245-47.

17
Emmons and de Laguna, *The Tlingit Indians*, 245.

18
Thomas Vaughn and Bill Holm, *Soft Gold*, 96.

19
Vaughn and Holm, *Soft Gold*, 87.

20
John R. Swanton, *Contributions to the Ethnology of the Haida Jesup North Pacific Expedition*, 92.

21
Palfray, Ives, Foote and Brown, Catalogue, East-India Marine Company of Salem. Salem: Salem Press, 1831.

22
From a conversation between the writer and Thomas Knowles, Director of Reference Services and Curator of Manuscripts, American Antiquarian Society, Worcester, Massachusetts, 1997.

23
The Log of Griffon, Phillips Library, Peabody Essex Museum, Salem (n.p., n.d.).

24
Mary Malloy, "Souvenirs of the Fur Trade 1799-1832: The Northwest Coast Collection of the Salem East India Marine Society," 30-76.

25
Bill Holm, "Will the Real Charles Edensaw Please Stand Up?: The Problem of Attribution in Northwest Coast Indian Art," 175-200; and Peter L. Macnair, Alan Hoover and Kevin Neary, *The Legacy: Continuing Traditions of Northwest Coast Indian Art*.

26
Robin Wright, "Two Haida Artists from Yan: Will Simeon Stilthda and John Gwaytihl Stand Apart," in progress. Wright's careful analysis sheds important additional light on the personal styles of these two Haida artists.

27
Swanton, *Haida Jesup North Pacific Expedition*, 13.

28
Franz Boas, *Tsimshian Mythology*, 454.

29
Franz Boas, *Kwakiutl Tales I*, 94.

30
Swanton, *Haida Jesup North Pacific Expedition*, 14.

31
The ceremonial objects and masks alienated by Indian Agent William Halliday in 1922 were sent to museums in Ottawa, Toronto and New York. Among the Kwakwaka'wakw, this regalia has come to be known as the "Potlatch Collection." Most of these heirlooms have since been returned and are at the U'mista Cultural Centre in Alert Bay and the Kwagiulth Museum at Cape Mudge.

32
Phil Nuytten, *The Totem Carvers: Charlie James, Ellen Neel, and Mungo Martin*.

33
Tolmie, *Physician and Fur Trader*, 292.

34
Boas, *Kwakiutl Tales I*, 34.

35
Swanton, *Haida Jesup North Pacific Expedition*, 17.

36
Earlier masks that served as models and inspiration for this one are in the Denver Art Museum collection, catalogue number 1953:402 (probably made by Charlie James) and in the Burke Museum in Seattle, catalogue number 1-1446 (which Mungo Martin identified as his own work in Holm, *Spirit and Ancestor*, 114). When Martin recounted the story of this mask, he used the Kwakwala term *kwakwani* (heron) to describe the bird; but when shown ornithological specimens, he was adamant that the bird intended was a sandhill crane. George Hunt Jr. represents a great blue heron in his version.

37
This mask and its attendant costume of fur are illustrated in Edward S. Curtis, *The Kwakiutl*, opposite page 184. The great grizzly mask of the Tlingit Shakes lineage has a similarly wondrous history, which is recorded in Holm, *Spirit and Ancestor*, 192.

38
Helen Abbott et al., eds., *The Spirit Within: Northwest Coast Native Art from the John H. Hauberg Collection*, 294.

39
Two examples in the collection of the Field Museum of Natural History, Chicago, also have this device. Hands are featured on the muzzle of the Nuḷamał mask (19242). An Echo mask (85815) with eleven interchangeable mouthpieces includes one which depicts a pair of hands emerging on either side of pursed lips. The carver, Bob Harris, identifies this mouthpiece as representing the Nuḷamał.

40
Curtis, *The Kwakiutl*, 156.

41
Swanton, *Haida Jesup North Pacific Expedition*, 26.

42
Steven C. Brown, "Formlines Changing Form: Northwest Coast Art as an Evolving Tradition," 62-83.

43
Nuytten, *The Totem Carvers*, 69.

SELECTED BIBLIOGRAPHY

Abbott, Donald N., ed. *The World Is As Sharp As a Knife: An Anthology in Honour of Wilson Duff*. Victoria: British Columbia Provincial Museum, 1981.

Abbott, Helen, et al., eds. *The Spirit Within: Northwest Coast Native Art from the John H. Hauberg Collection*. New York: Rizzoli International Publications, Inc., 1995.

Arima, Eugene. *The Westcoast (Nootka) People*. Special Publication 6. Victoria: British Columbia Provincial Museum, 1983.

Barnett, Homer G. "The Nature of the Potlatch," *American Anthropologist* 40 (1938):349-58.

Black, Martha. *Bella Bella: A Season of Heiltsuk Art*. Toronto: Royal Ontario Museum; Vancouver: Douglas & McIntyre, 1997.

Blackman, Margaret. *During My Time: Florence Edenshaw Davidson, A Haida Woman*. Seattle: University of Washington Press; Vancouver: Douglas & McIntyre, 1982.

Boas, Franz. *Ethnology of the Kwakiutl*. Bureau of American Ethnology Thirty-fifth Annual Report I and II. Washington: Smithsonian Institution, 1921.

Boas, Franz. *Facial Paintings of the Indians of Northern British Columbia*. American Museum of Natural History Memoirs 2. New York: American Museum of Natural History, 1898.

Boas, Franz. *Kwakiutl Ethnography*. Helen Codere, ed., Chicago: University of Chicago Press, 1966.

Boas, Franz. *Kwakiutl Tales I*. Contributions to Anthropology 26. New York: Columbia University, 1935.

Boas, Franz. *Primitive Art*. New York: Dover Publications, Inc., 1955.

Boas, Franz. *The Religion of the Kwakiutl Indians*. Columbia University Contributions to Anthropology 10, 1930. Reprint, New York: AMS Press Reprint, 1969.

Boas, Franz. *The Social Organization and the Secret Societies of the Kwakiutl Indians*. Report of the United States National Museum 1895. Washington: Smithsonian Institution Press, 1897.

Boas, Franz. *Tsimshian Mythology*. Thirty-first Annual Report of the Bureau of American Ethnology. Washington: Smithsonian Institution, 1916.

Brown, Steven C. "Formlines Changing Form: Northwest Coast Art as an Evolving Tradition," *American Indian Art Magazine* 22, no. 2 (1997):62ff.

Cole, Douglas. *Captured Heritage: The Scramble for Northwest Coast Artifacts*. Seattle: University of Washington Press; Vancouver: Douglas & McIntyre, 1985.

Curtis, Edward S. *The Kwakiutl*. The North American Indian, vol.10. 1915. Reprint, New York: Johnson Reprint, 1970.

Dauenhauer, Nora Marks. "Tlingit At.óow: Traditions and Concepts." In *The Spirit Within*. Seattle: Seattle Art Museum, 1995.

Dauenhauer, Nora Marks and Richard. *Haa Shuká: Our Ancestors*. Classics of Tlingit Oral Literature, vol. 1. Seattle: University of Washington Press, 1987.

Dauenhauer, Nora Marks and Richard. *Haa Tuwunáagu Yís: For Healing Our Spirit*. Classics of Tlingit Oral Literature, vol. 2. Seattle: University of Washington Press, 1990.

Dawson, George M. *On the Haida Indians of the Queen Charlotte Islands*. Reports of Explorations and Surveys Report of Progress for 1878-79. Montreal: Geological Survey of Canada, 1880.

de Laguna, Frederica. *Under Mount Saint Elias: The History and Culture of the Yakutat Tlingit*. Smithsonian Contributions to Anthropology 7. Washington: Smithsonian Institution, 1972.

Drucker, Philip. *Kwakiutl Dancing Societies*. Anthropological Records 2. Berkely and Los Angeles: University of California Press, 1940.

Drucker, Philip. *The Northern and Central Nootkan Tribes*. Bureau of American Ethnology Bulletin 144. Washington: Smithsonian Institution, 1951.

Duff, Wilson. *Arts of the Raven: Masterworks by the Northwest Coast Indian*. Vancouver: Vancouver Art Gallery, 1967.

Duff, Wilson. *Images Stone B.C.: Thirty Centuries of Northwest Coast Indian Sculpture*. Saanichton, B.C.: Hancock House, 1975.

Emmons, George T. *The Chilcat Blanket: Memoirs of the American Museum of Natural History*. Whole Series, vol. 3, Anthropology, vol. 4. New York: American Museum of Natural History, 1907.

Emmons, George T., and Frederica de Laguna, eds. *The Tlingit Indians*. Seattle: University of Washington Press; New York: American Museum of Natural History; Vancouver: Douglas & McIntyre, 1991.

Ernst, Alice H. *The Wolf Ritual of the Northwest Coast*. Eugene: University of Oregon Press, 1952.

Fladmark, Knut R. *British Columbia Prehistory*. Ottawa: National Museum of Man, 1986.

Goldman, Irving. *The Mouth of Heaven: An Introduction to Kwakiutl Religious Thought*. New York: John Wiley & Sons, 1975.

Gunther, Erna. *Indian Life on the Northwest Coast of North America*. Chicago: University of Chicago Press, 1972.

Halpin, Marjorie. " 'Seeing' in Stone: Tsimshian Masking and the Twin Stone Masks." In *The Tsimshian—Images of the Past: Views for the Present*. M. Seguin, ed. Vancouver: University of British Columbia Press, 1984.

Halpin, Marjorie. "The Tsimshian Crest System: A Study Based on Museum Specimens and the Marius Barbeau and William Beynon Field Notes." Ph.D. diss., University of British Columbia, 1973.

Hawthorn, Audrey. *Art of the Kwakiutl Indians and Other Northwest Coast Tribes*. Vancouver: University of British Columbia Press, 1967.

Hawthorn, Audrey. *Kwakiutl Art*. Seattle and London: University of Washington Press; Vancouver: Douglas & McIntyre, 1967.

Henry, John Frazier. *Early Maritime Artists of the Pacific Northwest Coast, 1741-1841*. Seattle and London: University of Washington Press, 1984.

Holm, Bill. *The Box of Daylight: Northwest Coast Indian Art*. Seattle: Seattle Art Museum and University of Washington Press; Vancouver: Douglas & McIntyre, 1983.

Holm, Bill. "Heraldic Carving Styles of the Northwest Coast." In *American Indian Art: Form and Tradition*. Minneapolis: Walker Art Center and the Minneapolis Institute of Art, 1972.

Holm, Bill. *Northwest Coast Indian Art: An Analysis of Form*. Thomas Burke Memorial Washington State Museum Monograph, no. 1. Seattle: University of Washington Press; Vancouver: Douglas & McIntyre, 1965.

Holm, Bill. *Smoky-Top: The Art and Times of Willie Seaweed*. Thomas Burke Memorial Washington State Museum Monograph, no.3. Seattle and London: University of Washington Press; Vancouver: Douglas & McIntyre, 1983.

Holm, Bill. *Spirit and Ancestor, A Century of Northwest Coast Indian Art at the Burke Museum*. Thomas Burke Memorial Washington State Museum Monograph, no. 4. Seattle: University of Washington Press; Vancouver: Douglas & McIntyre, 1987.

Holm, Bill. "Will the Real Charles Edensaw Please Stand Up?: The Problem of Attribution in Northwest Coast Indian Art." In *The World Is As Sharp As a Knife: An Anthology in Honour of Wilson Duff*. Donald N. Abbott, ed. Victoria: British Columbia Provincial Museum, 1981.

Jacobsen, Johan Adrian. *Alaskan Voyage 1881-1883: An Expedition to the Northwest Coast of America*. Erna Gunther, trans. Chicago: University of Chicago Press, 1977.

Jewitt, John. *The Adventures and Sufferings of John R. Jewitt, Captive Among the Nootka*. Toronto: McClelland & Stewart, 1974.

Jonaitis, Aldona. *Art of the Northern Tlingit*. Seattle and London: University of Washington Press, 1986.

Jonaitis, Aldona. *Chiefly Feasts: The Enduring Kwakiutl Potlatch*. Seattle: University of Washington Press; New York: American Museum of Natural History; Vancouver: Douglas & McIntyre, 1991.

Jonaitis, Aldona. *From the Land of the Totem Poles: The Northwest Coast Indian Art Collection at the American Museum of Natural History*. Seattle: University of Washington Press; New York: American Museum of Natural History; Vancouver: Douglas & McIntyre, 1988.

King, J. C. H. *Artificial Curiosities from the Northwest Coast of America*. London: British Museum, 1981.

Lévi-Strauss, Claude. *The Way of the Masks*. Seattle and London: University of Washington Press; Vancouver: Douglas & McIntyre, 1982.

MacDonald, George. *Haida Monumental Art*. Vancouver: University of British Columbia Press, 1983.

McIlwraith, T. F. *The Bella Coola Indians*. Toronto: University of Toronto Press, 1948.

Macnair, Peter L., and Alan Hoover. *The Magic Leaves: A History of Haida Argillite Carving*. Special Publication 7. Victoria: British Columbia Provincial Museum, 1984.

Macnair, Peter L., Alan Hoover and Kevin Neary. *The Legacy: Continuing Traditions of Northwest Coast Indian Art*. Victoria: British Columbia Provincial Museum, 1980.

Malloy, Mary. "Souvenirs of the Fur Trade 1799-1832: The Northwest Coast Collection of the Salem East India Marine Society," *American Indian Art Magazine* 11, no. 4 (1986):30-76.

Mitchell, Donald H. "Sebassa's Men." In *The World Is As Sharp As a Knife: An Anthology in Honour of Wilson Duff*. Donald N. Abbott, ed. Victoria: British Columbia Provincial Museum, 1981.

Mochon, Marion Johnson. *Masks of the Northwest Coast*. Milwaukee: Milwaukee Public Museum, 1966.

Niblack, Albert P. "The Coast Indians of Southern Alaska and Northern British Columbia." *Report of the United States National Museum 1888* 1890. Reprint, New York: Johnson Reprint, 1970.

Nuytten, Phil. *The Totem Carvers: Charlie James, Ellen Neel, and Mungo Martin*. Vancouver: Panorama Publications Ltd., 1982.

Olson, Ronald L. *Notes on the Bella Bella Kwakiutl*, Anthropological Records 14, no. 5 (1955):319-48.

Robinson, Michael P. *The Sea Otter Chiefs*. Calgary: Baycux Arts Inc., 1996.

Sawyer, Alan R. "Toward More Precise Northwest Coast Attributions: Two Substyles of Haisla Masks." In *The Box of Daylight: Northwest Coast Indian Art*. Seattle: University of Washington Press and the Seattle Art Museum, 1983.

Stott, Margaret A. *Bella Coola Ceremony and Art*. Canadian Ethnology Service Paper 21. Ottawa: National Museums of Canada, 1975.

Sturtevant, William C. *Boxes and Bowls: Decorated Containers by 19th Century Haida, Tlingit, Bella Bella, and Tsimshian Artists*. Washington: Smithsonian Institution, 1974.

Suttles, Wayne, ed. Northwest Coast. *Handbook of North American Indians*, vol. 7. Washington: Smithsonian Institution, 1990.

Swan, James G. *The Haidah Indians of Queen Charlotte's Islands*. Contribution of Knowledge 21. Washington: Smithsonian Institution, 1874.

Swanton, John R. *Contributions to the Ethnology of the Haida Jesup North Pacific Expedition* 5 no. 1. 1905. Reprint, New York: AMS Press Reprint, 1975.

Swanton, John R. *Tlingit Myths and Texts*. Bureau of American Ethnology Bulletin 39. Washington: Smithsonian Institution, 1909.

Thom, Ian. *Robert Davidson: Eagle of the Dawn*. Vancouver: Douglas & McIntyre and Vancouver Art Gallery, 1993.

Thomas, Susan. "The Life and Work of Charles Edenshaw: A Study of Innovation." Master's thesis, University of British Columbia, 1967.

Tolmie, William Fraser. *Physician and Fur Trader: The Journals of William Fraser Tolmie*. Vancouver: Mitchell Press, 1963.

Vancouver, George. *A Voyage of Discovery to the North Pacific Ocean and Round the World, 1791-1795*. W. Kaye Lamb ed. London: The Hakluyt Society, 1984.

Vaughn, Thomas, and Bill Holm. *Soft Gold, The Fur Trade & Cultural Exchange on the Northwest Coast of America*. Portland: Oregon Historical Society, 1982.

Walker Art Center. *American Indian Art: Form and Tradition*. Minneapolis: Walker Art Center and the Minneapolis Institute of Art, 1972.

Wright, E. W. ed. *Lewis & Dryden's Marine History of the Pacific Northwest*. Portland: The Lewis & Dryden Printing Company, 1895.

Wright, Robin K. "The Depiction of Women in Nineteenth Century Haida Argillite Carving," *American Indian Art Magazine* 11:4 (1986):36-45.

Wright, Robin K. "Haida Argillite—Made for Sale," *American Indian Art Magazine* 7 (1982):48-55.

Wright, Robin K. "Two Haida Artists from Yan: Will Simeon Stilthda and John Gwaytihl Stand Apart," *American Indian Art Magazine* 23:3 (1998):42-57, 106.

LIST OF WORKS IN THE EXHIBITION

The objects in this list have been ordered according to their attributed Nation of origin: that is, Tlingit, Nisga'a, Gitxsan, Tsimshian, Haida, Heiltsuk, Nuxalk, Kwakwaka'wakw, Nuu-chah-nulth, Makah. Within those divisions, the order is chronological.

Masks marked with an asterisk (*) indicate a new attribution for the artist, type or date. This attribution has been made by curator Peter Macnair. All measurements are in centimetres: height precedes width precedes depth.

Gitxsan

Artist Unknown
Naxnóx Mask Representing Human, 19th century
22.0 × 20.8 × 11.3
wood and paint
McMichael Canadian Art Collection, Kleinburg, 1969.28

Walter Harris
Headdress Representing Killer Whale, 1969
49.8 × 66.0 × 116.0
birch, hair, twine, copper and paint
Royal British Columbia Museum, Victoria, 13920

Walter Harris
Mask Representing Eagle Woman, 1969
71.5 × 24.4 × 13.6
birch, hair, twine, cedar bark, copper and paint
Royal British Columbia Museum, Victoria, 13918

Earl Muldoe
Forehead Mask Representing Wolf, 1969
19.6 × 19.1 × 41.8
birch, horsehair, leather, copper, bone and paint
Royal British Columbia Museum, Victoria, 13917

Haida

Artist Unknown
Labret, before 1794
2.0 × 8.0 × 5.0
wood
Peabody Museum of Archeology and Ethnology, Harvard University, Cambridge, 10/277

Artist Unknown
Mask Representing Killer Whale, 19th century
20.3 × 20.3 × 73.6
wood and paint
National Museum of Natural History, Smithsonian Institution, Washington, 89102

Artist Unknown
Mask Representing Djilakons, an Eagle Moiety Ancestor, before 1826
26.0 × 20.0 × 14.0
wood and paint
Peabody Museum of Archeology and Ethnology, Harvard University, Cambridge, 10/76826

Artist Unknown
Figure Representing Djilakons, c. 1830
20.0 × 8.5 × 5.5
wood, hair and paint
Peabody Museum of Archeology and Ethnology, Harvard University, Cambridge, 10/53093

Artist Unknown
Mask Representing Djilakons, c. 1830
19.5 × 15.0 × 5.5
wood and paint
Peabody Museum of Archeology and Ethnology, Harvard University, Cambridge, 10/51671

Artist Unknown
Mask Representing Djilakons, c. 1830
17.1 × 16.5 × 13.9
wood and paint
National Museum of Natural History, Smithsonian Institution, Washington, 2666

Artist Unknown
Mask Representing Noble Woman with Labret, before 1831
21.5 × 16.5 × 11.0
wood and paint
McCord Museum of Canadian History, Montréal, M10390

Artist Unknown
Mask Representing Male Ancestor, before 1840
26.03 × 20.3 × 12.7
wood and paint
National Museum of Natural History, Smithsonian Institution, Washington, 73332B

Artist Unknown
Mask Representing Young Woman, before 1840
22.9 × 18.4 × 11.4
wood, metal and paint
National Museum of Natural History, Smithsonian Institution, Washington, 2667

Artist Unknown
Mask Representing Woman with Labret, before 1840
24.1 × 19.1 × 11.4
wood and paint
National Museum of Natural History, Smithsonian Institution, Washington, 2665

Artist Unknown
Mask Representing Noble Woman Wearing Labret, c. 1840
20.9 × 22.9 × 11.1
wood, paint and glass beads
University of Pennsylvania Museum of Archaeology and Anthropology, Philadelphia, 45-15-2

Artist Unknown
Mask Representing Woman Wearing Labret, c. 1840
24.1 × 20.3 × 11.4
wood, abalone shell, copper, leather and paint
National Museum of Natural History, Smithsonian Institution, Washington, 89049

Artist Unknown
Mask Representing Male Ancestor, c. 1850, collected in 1879
26.5 × 21.5
wood, hide, bone, nails and paint
Canadian Museum of Civilization, Hull, VII-B-3

Artist Unknown
Mask Representing Male Ancestor, c. 1850, collected in 1884 at Masset
24.1 × 20.3
wood, copper, hide and paint
Canadian Museum of Civilization, Hull, VII-B-1554

Artist Unknown
Mask Representing Puffin, c. 1860
27.0 × 21.5 × 55.5
wood and paint
McCord Museum of Canadian History, Montréal, ME892.20

Artist Unknown
Mask Representing Young Woman, c. 1860
20.8 × 17.3 × 9.2
wood, abalone shell and paint
Canadian Museum of Civilization, Hull VII-B-928 a,b

Simeon Stilthda*
Transformation Mask, c. 1865
22.8 × 45.7 × 58.4
wood, pigment, hide and metal
American Museum of Natural History, New York, 16/376

Simeon Stilthda*
Mask Representing Elderly Man, c. 1870
23.2 × 20.2 × 11.0
wood, hide, fur, nails, string and paint
Royal British Columbia Museum, Victoria, 10670

Simeon Stilthda*
Mask Representing Elderly Noble Woman, c. 1870
23.0 × 20.2 × 11.0
wood, abalone shell, leather and string
Royal British Columbia Museum, Victoria, 10671

Simeon Stilthda*
Mask Representing Elderly Woman, c. 1870
23.6 × 18.4 × 11.4
wood, abalone shell, leather, string and paint
McMichael Canadian Art Collection, Kleinburg, 1981.103

Simeon Stilthda*
Mask Representing Young Man, c. 1870
24.1 × 20.6 × 11.6
wood, hide, nails and paint
Royal British Columbia Museum, Victoria, 10665

Simeon Stilthda*
Mask Representing Young Woman, c. 1870
22.5 × 18.0 × 10.2
wood, string, metal and paint
Royal British Columbia Museum, Victoria, 10666

Artist Unknown
Mask Representing Supernatural Being, collected 1879
25.5 × 19.0
wood, copper, hair, hide and paint
Canadian Museum of Civilization, Hull, VII-B-10

Artist Unknown
Mask Representing Bear, c. 1880
53.5 × 38.2 × 16.0
wood and paint
Royal British Columbia Museum, Victoria, 1419

John Gwaytihl
Mask Representing Young Woman Wearing Training Labret, 1882
29.2 × 46.2 × 61.7
wood, metal and paint
American Museum of Natural History, New York, 16/364

John Cross
Mask Representing Eagle Down Woman, c. 1900
30.3 × 29.8 × 14.8
wood, nails and paint
Vancouver Museum, Vancouver, AA93

Charles Edenshaw
Mask Representing Gagiit, c. 1905
53.3 × 76.2
wood, hair, string and paint
American Museum of Natural
History, New York, 16.1/128

Freda Diesing
*Mask Representing Elderly Noble
Woman*, 1974
23.5 × 21.3 × 11.0
birch, red cedar bark, hair,
abalone shell, buckskin and glass
beads
Royal British Columbia Museum,
Victoria, 15057

Robert Davidson
*Mask Representing Woman Wearing
Labret*, 1975
20.5 × 15.0 × 10.5
alder, abalone shell and paint
Private Collection

Robert Davidson
Mask Representing Eagle Spirit,
1980
22.8 × 22.3 × 15.5
red cedar, maple, hide, feathers,
brass, leather, opercula and paint
Private Collection

Guujaaw
Mask Representing Raven, 1980
20.0 × 77.0 × 18.5
red cedar, cedar bark, cloth, cedar
branches, feathers, leather, nails,
nylon twine and paint
Private Collection

Reg Davidson
Mask Representing Eagle Ancestor,
1983
26.5 × 22.5 × 18.0
red cedar, abalone shell, copper,
hair and paint
Private Collection

Robert Davidson
Mask Representing Gagiit, 1983
34.0 × 37.5 × 24.0
red cedar, horsehair, screws, cloth
and paint
Private Collection

Robert Davidson
Mask Representing Shark, 1986
82.0 × 57.5 × 38.0
red cedar, copper, horsehair,
opercula, abalone shell, leather,
aluminum, yew and paint
Private Collection

Reg Davidson
Mask Representing Gagiit, c. 1988
31.0 × 33.5 × 24.0
red cedar, horsehair, opercula and
paint
Private Collection

Reg Davidson
*Mask Representing Raven and
Dogfish*, c. 1990
50.0 × 21.0 × 25.0
red cedar, cedar bark, opercula,
nails, twine and paint
Private Collection

Heiltsuk

Artist Unknown
*Mask Combining Raven and
Killerwhale Elements*, 19th century
25.4 × 27.9 × 104.1
wood, hair, copper and paint
National Museum of Natural
History, Smithsonian Institution,
Washington, 89043

Artist Unknown
Mask Representing Male Ancestor,
c. 1845*
23.5 × 19.1 × 11.4
wood, hide, nails and paint
National Museum of Natural
History, Smithsonian Institution,
Washington, 688

Artist Unknown
*Mask Representing Personified
Moon*, c. 1850
31.7 × 58.4 × 66.0
wood, pigment, hide, abalone
shell and paint
American Museum of Natural
History, New York, 16/594

Artist Unknown
Headdress Mask Representing Eagle,
c. 1860*
15.2 × 55.9 × 116.8
wood, copper, hide, opercula and
paint
National Museum of Natural
History, Smithsonian Institution,
Washington, 20571

Artist Unknown
*Mask Representing Ancestral
Human*, c. 1860
29.5 × 27.5 × 16.5
wood and paint
McCord Museum of Canadian
History, Montréal, ME982.32.3

Artist Unknown
Mask Representing Sculpin, c. 1860
27.9 × 53.3 × 111.8
wood, canvas, copper, iron and
paint
National Museum of Natural
History, Smithsonian Institution,
Washington, 20573

Artist Unknown
Transformation Mask, c. 1865
33.0 × 38.0 × 68.5
wood, hair, leather and paint
Canadian Museum of
Civilization, Hull, VII-B-20

Artist Unknown
Mask Representing Cannibal Bird,
c. 1865
48.0 × 29.2 × 149.0
red cedar, iron and paint
Royal British Columbia Museum,
Victoria, 8

Artist Unknown
Mask Representing Male Ancestor,
c. 1865*
28.0 × 28.8 × 15.0
wood and paint
Canadian Museum of
Civilization, Hull, VII-D-25

Artist Unknown
Cannibal Bird Mask, c. 1870
72.3 × 58.4 × 137.1
wood, bear fur, cord and paint
American Museum of Natural
History, New York, 16/963

Artist Unknown
*Mask Representing Ancestral
Human*, c. 1870
27.0 × 23.5 × 14.5
wood and paint
McCord Museum of Canadian
History, Montréal, ME982.32.1

Artist Unknown
Mask Representing Pkvs, c. 1880
50.1 × 32.0 × 20.7
wood, horsehair, leather, nails
and paint
McMichael Canadian Art
Collection, Kleinburg, 1984.5

Kwakwaka'wakw

Artist Unknown
Mask Representing Ancestral Sun,
19th century
43.8 × 41.5 × 18.5
cedar, nails and paint
Royal British Columbia Museum,
Victoria, 10243

Artist Unknown
Mask Representing Sea Lion, 19th
century
34.9 × 21.6 × 28.6
red cedar, sea lion whiskers and
paint
University of Pennsylvania
Museum of Archaeology and
Anthropology, Philadelphia, 29-
175-34

Artist Unknown
Forehead Mask Representing Wolf,
c. 1840
55.8 × 55.8 × 83.8
wood, pigment and hair
American Museum of Natural
History, New York, 16/8200

Artist Unknown
Mask Representing Grizzly Bear,
c. 1840
26.0 × 26.7 × 42.8
red cedar, bearskin, sinew, glass
and paint
Royal British Columbia Museum,
Victoria, 9187

Artist Unknown
Mask Representing Nuḷamaḷ,
c. 1840
27.8 × 20.0 × 16.6
wood and paint
Royal British Columbia Museum,
Victoria, 15981

Artist Unknown
Mask Representing Nuḷamaḷ,
c. 1840
35.5 × 22.5 × 15.0
wood and paint
Staatliche Museen zu Berlin—
Preußischer Kulturbesitz
Museum für Völkerkunde, Berlin,
IV-A524

Artist Unknown
Forehead Mask Representing Wolf,
c. 1860
48.2 × 48.2 × 92.7
wood, hair and paint
American Museum of Natural
History, New York, 16/384

Artist Unknown
Forehead Mask Representing Wolf,
c. 1860
17.8 × 19.0 × 41.9
wood, hair, feathers, cedar bark
and paint
National Museum of Natural
History, Smithsonian Institution,
Washington, 274261

Artist Unknown
Mask Representing Dzunukwa, late
19th century
58.0 × 42.2 × 24.0
red cedar, mirrors, fur, nails and
paint
U'mista Cultural Centre, Alert
Bay, 80.01.133

Artist Unknown
Mask Representing Nuḷamaḷ,
c. 1870
36.0 × 23.0 × 13.5
wood and paint
Royal Ontario Museum, Toronto,
HN386

Artist Unknown
Chief's Dzunukwa Mask, c. 1880
27.5 × 23.5 × 13.7
wood, human hair, bear skin and
paint
Campbell River Museum,
Campbell River, 994.7

Artist Unknown
Mask Representing Bakwas, c. 1880
37.1 × 27.0 × 20.4
red cedar, horsehair, nails and
paint
Royal British Columbia Museum,
Victoria, 1913

Artist Unknown
Mask Representing Dzunukwa,
c. 1880
50.8 × 40.6 × 33.0
wood, hair, hide, nails and paint
Milwaukee Public Museum,
Milwaukee, 17359

Artist Unknown
Mask Representing Kumugwe',
c. 1880
48.9 × 43.2 × 15.2
alder, red cedar bark, cloth and
paint
Gift of John H. Hauberg, Seattle
Art Museum, Seattle, 91.1.30

Artist Unknown
Ridicule Mask, c. 1885
27.4 × 17.4 × 7.0
wood and paint
National Museum of the
American Indian, New York,
6/8833

Artist Unknown
Mask Representing Bakwas, c. 1890
33.0 × 21.6 × 26.7
wood, hide, fur, nails and paint
Milwaukee Public Museum,
Milwaukee, 17361

Artist Unknown
Mask Representing Nuḷamaḷ,
c. 1890
46.0 × 28.0 × 23.0
red cedar, hair and paint
Royal British Columbia Museum,
Victoria, 1914

Bond Sound
Chief's Dzunuḵwa Mask, c. 1890
27.4 × 23.0 × 25.5
hemlock, human hair, twine,
baleen and paint
Royal British Columbia Museum,
Victoria, 12924

Bob Harris*
Mask Representing Baḵwas, c. 1890
30.5 × 25.5 × 25.0
red cedar, horsehair, feathers,
brass and cloth
U'mista Cultural Centre, Alert
Bay, 80.01.013

Charlie James*
Mask Representing Bagwis, c. 1900
31.8 × 24.1 × 34.3
wood, cedar bark, paint and nails
Milwaukee Public Museum,
Milwaukee, 17320

Charlie James*
*Transformation Mask Representing
Ancestral Sun*, c. 1910
75.0 × 67.0 × 35.0
red cedar, cotton twine, leather,
nails and paint
Royal British Columbia Museum,
Victoria, 1908

Charlie James*
Mask Representing Sun, c. 1915
40.5 × 35.2 × 24.5
red cedar, cotton twine, rubber
and paint
U'mista Cultural Centre, Alert
Bay, 80.01.131

Willie Seaweed
Mask Representing a Speaker,
c. 1930
28.5 × 19.0 × 14.0
yellow cedar and paint
Campbell River Museum,
Campbell River, 992.13

Willie Seaweed
*Mask Representing Husband of
Birthing Woman*, c. 1930
30.5 × 20.3 × 12.7
red cedar and paint
University of British Columbia,
Museum of Anthropology,
Vancouver, A6238

Willie Seaweed
*Mask Representing Woman Giving
Birth*, c. 1930
30.5 × 20.3 × 12.7
red cedar, cotton twine and paint
University of British Columbia,
Museum of Anthropology,
Vancouver, A6237

Willie Seaweed
Xwixwi Mask, c. 1930
22.8 × 17.7 × 34.2
red cedar and paint
University of British Columbia,
Museum of Anthropology,
Vancouver, A3662

Willie Seaweed
Xwixwi Mask, c. 1930
24.7 × 15.2 × 33.02
red cedar and paint
University of British Columbia,
Museum of Anthropology,
Vancouver, A4095

Willie Seaweed
Mask Representing Crooked-Beak,
c. 1940
103.0 × 29.0 × 90.0
red cedar, cedar bark, nails,
leather, twine and paint
Royal British Columbia Museum,
Victoria, 17377

Willie Seaweed
Mask Representing Crooked-Beak,
c. 1954
73.6 × 30.5 × 10.0
red cedar, wood, cedar bark,
cotton twine, nails and paint
University of British Columbia,
Museum of Anthropology,
Vancouver, A8327

Mungo Martin
Mask Representing Echo, c. 1955
30.9 × 29.9 × 35.0
red cedar
Royal British Columbia Museum,
Victoria, 16512

Ellen Neel
Mask Representing Dzunuḵwa,
c. 1955
24.0 × 19.0 × 15.5
red cedar
Private Collection

Mungo Martin
*Mask Representing Supernatural
Sandhill Crane*, c. 1956
102.0 × 157.0 × 42.5
red cedar, cotton twine, nails and
paint
Royal British Columbia Museum,
Victoria, 9250

Henry Hunt
*Mask Representing Killer Whale
Man*, 1960
31.0 × 26.0 × 24.0
red cedar
Royal British Columbia Museum,
Victoria, 9411

Tony Hunt
Mask Representing Male Ancestor,
1967
26.1 × 20.4 × 15.6
red cedar and paint
Royal British Columbia Museum,
Victoria, 18913

Henry Hunt
Mask Representing Sea Monster,
1970
31.6 × 28.7 × 20.7
red cedar, copper and paint
Royal British Columbia Museum,
Victoria, 13215

Doug Cranmer
Mask Representing Huxwhukw,
1971
27.4 × 26.0 × 180.0
red cedar, cedar bark, leather,
nails, twine and paint
Royal British Columbia Museum,
Victoria, 13948

Richard Hunt
Mask Representing Ancestral Sun,
1978
50.5 × 58.0 × 20.0
red cedar, nylon twine, screws
and paint
Private Collection

Richard Hunt
Mask Representing Gadaxanis, 1978
26.0 × 20.0 × 17.7
red cedar, eagle feathers and
paint
Royal British Columbia Museum,
Victoria, 15993

Richard Hunt
Mask Representing Gadaxanis, 1978
28.7 × 20.2 × 18.2
red cedar, eagle feathers and
paint
Royal British Columbia Museum,
Victoria, 15994

Richard Hunt
Mask Representing Gadaxanis, 1978
23.5 × 20.1 × 15.2
red cedar, eagle feathers and
paint
Royal British Columbia Museum,
Victoria, 15995

Richard Hunt
Mask Representing Gadaxanis, 1978
26.2 × 19.2 × 18.4
red cedar, eagle feathers and
paint
Royal British Columbia Museum,
Victoria, 15996

Richard Hunt
Mask Representing Gadaxanis, 1978
24.5 × 20.8 × 21.7
red cedar, eagle feathers and
paint
Royal British Columbia Museum,
Victoria, 15997

Richard Hunt
Mask Representing Gadaxanis, 1978
29.4 × 20.7 × 15.0
red cedar, eagle feathers and
paint
Royal British Columbia Museum,
Victoria, 15998

Richard Hunt
Mask Representing Gadaxanis, 1978
25.7 × 19.4 × 19.2
red cedar, eagle feathers and
paint
Royal British Columbia Museum,
Victoria, 15999

Richard Hunt
Mask Representing Gadaxanis, 1978
32.2 × 22.9 × 22.2
red cedar, eagle feathers and
paint
Royal British Columbia Museum,
Victoria, 16000

Richard Hunt
Mask Representing Killer Whale,
1978
58.0 × 60.0 × 1925.0
red cedar, nylon twine, leather,
nails and paint
Royal British Columbia Museum,
Victoria, 16460

Mervyn Child
Raven Transformation Mask, 1980
35.0 × 79.0 × 61.0
red cedar, horsehair, cloth, nylon
twine, plastic lens and paint
Private Collection

Tony Hunt
Mask Representing Crooked-Beak,
1980
77.0 × 25.0 × 94.0
red cedar, cedar bark, raffia,
leather, nails, nylon twine and
paint
Private Collection

Tony Hunt
Mask Representing Huxwhukw,
1980
38.0 × 29.0 × 180.0
red cedar, cedar bark, brass nails,
nylon twine and leather
Private Collection

Beau Dick
*Mask Representing Long Life
Bringer*, 1982
39.5 × 23.0 × 14.0
alder, cedar bark, twine, rubber
and paint
Private Collection

Calvin Hunt
Thunderbird Costume, 1982
200.6 × 124.4 × 78.7
cedar, cedar bark, canvas, feath-
ers, nails and paint
University of British Columbia,
Museum of Anthropology,
Vancouver, 863/1-4

Henry Speck
Mask Representing Crooked-Beak,
1983
55.0 × 28.0 × 101.0
red cedar, cedar bark, nylon
twine, leather and paint
Collection of Dr. Granger Avery
and Mrs. Winnie Avery

Mervyn Child
Mask Representing Baḵwas, 1985
30.0 × 34.0 × 21.0
red cedar, horsehair, cloth, nails,
nylon twine and paint
Private Collection

Beau Dick
*Mask Featuring Four Cannibal
Birds*, c. 1985
81.0 × 44.0 × 105.5
red cedar, yellow cedar, cedar
bark, nails, twine, leather and
paint
Private Collection

Beau Dick
Mask Representing Laugher,
c. 1985
31.0 × 26.5 × 14.5
red cedar, cedar bark, nails,
twine, feathers and paint
Private Collection

Tom Hunt
Forehead Mask Representing Kulus,
1985
30.5 × 44.5 × 23.0
red cedar, yellow cedar, cedar
bark and paint
Private Collection

Henry Speck
Mask Representing Huxwhukw,
c. 1985
22.0 × 26.0 × 151.0
red cedar, cedar bark, leather,
nails, wire, nylon twine and paint
Private Collection

Tony Hunt Jr.
*Mask Representing 'Namgis
Ancestor,* 1987
69.0 × 60.0 × 27.0
red cedar, copper, nylon twine,
maple, crystal and paint
Royal British Columbia Museum,
Victoria, 18651

George Hunt Jr.
Mask Representing Crooked-Beak,
1989
88.0 × 93.0 × 24.0
red cedar, cedar bark, horsehair,
copper, abalone shell, leather,
nylon twine and paint
Private Collection

Tony Hunt Jr.
Xwixwi Mask, 1989
46.5 × 35.3 × 19.5
red cedar, cloth, cord, nails and
paint
Royal British Columbia Museum,
Victoria, 18983

Tony Hunt Jr.
Xwixwi Mask, 1989
50.5 × 42.5 × 19.5
red cedar, cloth, cord, nails and
paint
Royal British Columbia Museum,
Victoria, 18984

George Hunt Jr.
*Mask Representing Heron and
Kumugwe',* 1990
103.0 × 150.0 × 104.0
red cedar, yellow cedar, horsehair,
cedar bark, rope, nylon twine,
canvas, copper, abalone shell,
screws, nails, feathers and paint
Pegasus Gallery, Salt Spring
Island

Bill Henderson
Mask Representing Huxwhukw,
1991
38.0 × 33.0 × 168.0
red cedar, alder, cedar bark,
leather, nails, screws, staples,
nylon twine and paint
Private Collection

Wayne Alfred
*Mask Representing Raven Fin Killer
Whale,* 1992
61.0 × 33.0 × 152.5
red cedar, cedar bark, nylon
twine, leather, nails and paint
Private Collection

Wayne Alfred
*Mask Representing Transformation
Salmon,* 1992
43.0 × 121.0 × 43.0
red cedar, cedar bark, cloth,
nylon twine, nails, hinges and
paint
Private Collection

Kevin Cranmer
Forehead Mask Representing Kulus,
1992
29.5 × 22.0 × 68.0
red cedar, leather, nails, rabbit
fur, feathers, cloth, nylon twine
and paint
Private Collection

Simon Dick
Forehead Mask Representing Wolf,
1992
60.9 × 27.0 × 23.0
red cedar, yellow cedar, horsehair,
wolf fur, styrofoam and paint
Private Collection

Simon Dick
Mask Representing a Heron, 1992
35.5 × 21.5 × 111.7
red cedar, horsehair, copper, brass
and paint
Private Collection

Bill Henderson
Mask Representing Crooked-Beak,
1992
65.0 × 28.0 × 76.0
red cedar, cedar bark, leather,
nails, twine and paint
Private Collection

Calvin Hunt
Mask Representing Moon and Eagle,
1993
67.0 × 65.5 × 22.0
red cedar, copper, abalone shell,
screws, nails and paint
Private Collection

Henry Speck
Mask Representing Cannibal Raven,
1993
35.0 × 25.5 × 123.0
red cedar, cedar bark, leather,
nails, nylon twine and paint
Collection of Dr. Granger Avery
and Mrs. Winnie Avery

Joe Wilson
*Mask Representing Chief's
Dzunukwa,* 1994
28.0 × 22.0 × 14.0
red cedar, horsehair, black bear
fur, nails, nylon twine, leather
and paint
Private Collection

Tom Hunt
*Forehead Mask Representing
Supernatural Copper Frog,* 1995
24.2 × 39.5 × 40.5
red cedar, paint
Private Collection

Stan Wamiss
Triple Transformation Mask, 1997
50.5 × 61.0 × 97.5 (closed)
red cedar, veneer, plywood, hair,
hinges, twine and paint
Private Collection

Tom Hunt
Mask Representing Bakwas, 1998
35.5 × 22.8 × 20.3
red cedar, cedar bark and paint
Private Collection

Joe Wilson
*Mask Representing 'Namgis
Ancestor,* 1998
77.0 × 45.0 × 34.0
red cedar, cedar bark, cloth,
nylon twine, hemlock branches,
shell beads, metal bells and paint
Campbell River Museum,
Campbell River, no accession
number

Makah

Artist Unknown
Mask Representing Woman, c. 1880
27.9 × 30.5 × 11.4
wood, hair, yarn and string
National Museum of Natural
History, Smithsonian Institution,
Washington, 4118

Greg Colfax
Mask Representing Pukubts, 1990
30.5 × 21.6 × 20.5
alder, cedar bark, horsetail, red
cloth, graphite and paint
Legacy Gallery, Seattle

Greg Colfax
Mask Representing Ancestor, 1998
27.9 × 22.8 × 19.0
alder, horsehair, cedar bark, cotton cloth and acrylic paint
Private Collection

Nisga'a

Artist Unknown
Mask Representing Moon, 19th
century
35.4 × 25.6 × 15.3
cedar, nails and paint
Royal British Columbia Museum,
Victoria, 9694

Artist Unknown
Naxnóx Mask, 19th century
26.5 × 25.2 × 21.7
red cedar, copper, nails, fur and
paint
Royal British Columbia Museum,
Victoria, 14308

Artist Unknown
*Naxnóx Mask Representing
Skimsim,* 19th century
29.7 × 26.7 × 33.6
cedar, nails, paint, red cedar and
bark
Royal British Columbia Museum,
Victoria, 1505

Artist Unknown
*Mask Representing Conceited White
Woman,* c. 1870
22.9 × 20.4 × 13.6
wood and paint
Royal British Columbia Museum,
Victoria, 9913

Norman Tait
Mask Representing Moon, 1983
19.6 × 21.7 × 7.0
wood and paint
Royal Ontario Museum, Toronto,
983.120.1

Nuu-chah-nulth

Artist Unknown
Mask Representing Male Ancestor,
18th century
20.7 × 17.3 × 12.5
wood and paint
Museum für Völkerkunde,
Vienna, 293

Artist Unknown
Mask Representing Spirit Ancestor,
18th Century
28.0 × 22.0 × 15.0
wood and paint
Bernisches Historisches Museum,
Bern, A1.13

Artist Unknown
Mask Representing Male, early 19th
century
16.0 × 14.5 × 8.0
wood and paint
Canadian Museum of
Civilization, Hull, VII-F-230

Artist Unknown
Xwixwi Mask, late 19th century
46.4 × 42.8 × 25.4
wood and paint
University of Pennsylvania
Museum of Archaeology and
Anthropology, Philadelphia,
29-175-29

Artist Unknown
Xwixwi Mask, late 19th century
55.9 × 40.6 × 25.4
wood and paint
University of Pennsylvania
Museum of Archaeology and
Anthropology, Philadelphia,
29-175-31

Artist Unknown
Mask Representing Male, c. 1870
32.0 × 23.0 × 24.0
wood, cedar bark, feathers and
paint
Canadian Museum of
Civilization, Hull, VII-F-923

Artist Unknown
Mask Representing Male Ancestor,
c. 1870
36.7 × 32.5 × 27.6
wood and paint
Canadian Museum of
Civilization, Hull, VII-F-385

Artist Unknown
Mask Representing Thunderbird,
c. 1870
21.0 × 18.0 × 33.0
red cedar, cedar bark, cloth, nails
and paint
Staatliche Museen zu Berlin—
Preußischer Kulturbesitz
Museum für Völkerkunde, Berlin,
IV-A7149

Clayoquot Artist*
Mask Representing Male Ancestor,
c. 1870
30.0 × 19.0
wood, hair and paint
Canadian Museum of
Civilization, Hull, VII-C-2

Cheletus*
Salmon Mask, c. 1880
75.0 × 29.0 × 33.0
cedar, cedar bark, cloth, feathers
and paint
Field Museum, Chicago, 85844

Artist Unknown
Mask Representing Pookmis, c. 1890
90.0 × 26.0 × 42.0
red cedar, cedar bark, fur, feather
and paint
Field Museum, Chicago, 85843

Ron Hamilton
*Mask Representing Ch'ihaa
(Ancestor)*, c. 1970
23.0 × 16.5 × 18.0
alder and paint
Private Collection

Ron Hamilton
Mask Representing Moon, c. 1975
40.6 × 35.6 × 17.8
red cedar and paint
Private Collection

Joe David
Mask Representing Ancestor, 1976
27.9 × 18.0 × 17.7
red cedar and paint
Royal British Columbia Museum,
Victoria, 14981

Art Thompson
*Mask Representing Thunderbird in
Human Form*, 1986
33.0 × 23.0 × 21.0
red cedar, copper, rope, red cedar
bark and paint
Royal British Columbia Museum,
Victoria, 18293

Joe David
Mask Representing Woman,
before 1987
17.5 × 14.0 × 22.0
wood, hair and paint
University of British Columbia,
Museum of Anthropology,
Vancouver, NB11.298

Art Thompson
*Mask Representing Thunderbird in
Human Form*, 1989
63.0 × 26.0 × 26.0
red cedar, cedar bark, eagle feathers, horsehair, copper, leather,
nylon twine, plywood, screws and
paint
Spirit Wrestler Gallery,
Vancouver

Art Thompson
Mask Representing Warrior, 1989
63.0 × 23.5 × 25.0
red cedar, alder, cedar bark,
horsehair, leather, nails, twine,
copper and paint
Spirit Wrestler Gallery,
Vancouver

Tim Paul
*Mask Representing November
Moon*, 1996
54.0 × 49.0 × 22.0
red cedar and paint
Collection of Dr. C. Schulz and
Dr. J. Striegel

Tim Paul
Mask Representing Pookmis, 1998
35.5 × 20.3 × 22.9
red cedar, cedar bark, feathers
and paint
Private Collection

Nuxalk

Artist Unknown
Sun Transformation Mask, c. 1865
100.0 diameter
wood, hair, twine and paint
Linden-Museum Stuttgart—
Staatliches Museum für
Völkerkunde, Stuttgart, 19178

Artist Unknown
*Mask Representing Sun**, c. 1870
160.0 diameter
wood and paint
American Museum of Natural
History, New York, 16/1507

Artist Unknown
*Mask Representing Sun**, c. 1870
39.0 × 35.0
wood and paint
Canadian Museum of
Civilization, Hull, VII-B-19

Artist Unknown
Mask Representing Spirit Creature,
c. 1880
30.5 × 20.3 × 21.6
alder, cedar bark, hair, cloth,
twine, nails and paint
Gift of John H. Hauberg, Seattle
Art Museum, Seattle, 91.1.34

Glenn Tallio
Mask Representing Thunder, 1990
30.0 × 24.0 × 24.5
red cedar, cedar bark, spruce
root, baleen and paint
Private Collection

Tlingit

Artist Unknown
Mask, 19th century
25.4 × 21.6 × 11.4
wood, hair, opercula, brass coins
and paint
National Museum of Natural
History, Smithsonian Institution,
Washington, 76855

Artist Unknown
*Mask Representing Humanoid
Eagle*, c. 1840
38.1 × 57.1 × 62.2
wood, pigment, opercula and
abalone shell
American Museum of Natural
History, New York, 19/852

Artist Unknown
Headdress Mask, c. 1850
8.8 × 22.8 × 26.1
wood and paint
American Museum of Natural
History, New York, E/1376

Artist Unknown
Headdress Mask, c. 1850
22.8 × 27.9 × 34.2
wood, pigment, abalone shell and
metal
American Museum of Natural
History, New York, 19/918

Artist Unknown
Mask, c. 1850
31.7 × 48.2 × 52.0
wood, pigment and hide
American Museum of Natural
History, New York, 16.1/996

Artist Unknown
Mask Representing Human Face,
c. 1850, collected before 1867
22.2 × 20.3 × 11.4
alder, hide and paint
Gift of John H. Hauberg, Seattle
Art Museum, Seattle, 91.1.118

Artist Unknown
Figure Representing Man, c. 1870*
17.8 × 8.9 × 9.2
wood and paint
National Museum of Natural
History, Smithsonian Institution,
Washington, 13102

Artist Unknown
Forehead Mask Representing Wolf,
c. 1880
43.2 × 20.3 × 26.7
wood, hair, copper, opercula,
cloth and paint
Portland Art Museum, Portland,
48.3.415

Tsimshian

Artist Unknown
Stone Mask, 19th century
22.5 × 24.0 × 18.2
stone and paint
Canadian Museum of
Civilization, Hull, VII-C-329

Artist Unknown
*Naxnóx Mask Representing
Human*, 19th century
23.1 × 18.3 × 7.9
wood and paint
McMichael Canadian Art
Collection, Kleinburg, 1978.21.2

Artist Unknown
*Naxnóx Mask Representing
Woman*, 19th century
22.5 × 20.8 × 11.3
wood, abalone shell and paint
McMichael Canadian Art
Collection, Kleinburg, 1979.5

Artist Unknown
*Mask Representing Moon**, c. 1850
30.5 × 33.0 × 15.2
wood and paint
Canadian Museum of
Civilization, Hull, VII-B-9

Artist Unknown
*Mask Representing Ancestral
Human*, c. 1860
26.2 × 20.0 × 14.0
wood and paint
McCord Museum of Canadian
History, Montréal, ME892.32.2

Artist Unknown
*Mask Representing Young Girl with
Braids*, c. 1860
30.8 × 20.6 × 14.0
wood, hair, cedar bark, twine and
paint
Portland Art Museum, Portland,
46.14

Artist Unknown
*Human Face Mask Representing
Male*, c. 1870
23.2 × 19.1 × 12.7
wood and paint
Gift of John H. Hauberg, Seattle
Art Museum, Seattle, 91.1.39

Artist Unknown
Mask Representing Male, c. 1870
21.0 × 16.5 × 9.5
wood and paint
Canadian Museum of
Civilization, Hull, VII-C-314

Artist Unknown
Mask Representing Naxnóx Spirit,
c. 1870
23.0 × 28.0 × 23.0
wood, copper, hair and paint
Canadian Museum of
Civilization, Hull, VII-C-1804